A few words about Darren Mitchell

"Thank you so much for talking to our class! You really inspired me and I loved the first chapter. It was great how you used memories to write scenes."
Mariah

"It was so fun hearing you talk about your book.
I can't wait to see it published!"
Scarlett

"Thank you for coming and answering our questions!
And thank you for the advice on not giving up on our dream to write and to stop making excuses."
Annie

"Thank you so much for taking the time to share your knowledge with us! I loved listening to how you got started becoming a writer, you were very inspirational.
I am excited to read the rest of your book."
Tess

"Your words really stuck with me. I can't wait to read more!"
Jencyn

"Thank you for taking your time to share your experience with us! You made me want to write more."
Suzy Diaz

"I really like where your books inspiration and I like your piece
of advice on keep writing and write whatever comes to mind.
I'm actually writing a story too for a show I might make.
I got more inspiration from you so I can finish that story."
Henry Davis Jr

"Thank you for coming to talk to us!
I'm gonna buy a copy on release!"
Miguel R.

"Maikai Ka hana ma ka puke
Good job on the book, keep up the work and mahalo
for coming to our class"
Malialani

"Yuh, I loved your ideas, they were so slay."
Jacob Serrano

"I am soooo reading your book and I can't wait for more
books to come out. But please consider romance, lol"
The Wolf Girl, Yonelle

I S A

Rising Darkness in Andalusia

Darren Mitchell

PAUL SMITH PUBLISHING
London

Published by Paul Smith Publishing London 2023

Cover Design Valentina Cheshenko 2022

The author asserts moral rights

A CIP catalogue record for this title is available from the British Library

ISBN PB 978-1-912597-20-8
ISBN eBook 978-1-912597-21-5

Paul Smith Publishing
www.paulsmithpublishing.co.uk

For Kaylie

May you follow your dreams with passion

Contents

1

Awakening

Slowly she opened her eyes. All around her was darkness. A howling in the distance sent shivers down into her core and she dared not move until her eyes began adjusting to the dark and she could make out trees. Her head hurt so bad, she put her hand to her head and felt a bump. "What happened?" Her body ached all over, but she forced herself to her feet leaning against a tree for support. She managed to stand despite her legs being shaky. I must think she said to herself. Where am I? How did I end up here?

The first rays of sunlight were beginning to penetrate the darkness. She climbed to the top of the tree and looked across the treetops. The brilliant multi-colored leaves seemed to go on forever. The moist morning air filled her lungs and calmed her. She stretched out her hand, the sun was so warm, but she still couldn't remember a thing. "I don't know this place. I'll wait here till the light breaks through the trees and then explore the area," she said aloud.

The howling grew closer until it was right below her and became a terrible wailing. What kind of creature makes such a horrible noise!? she thought and though scared, she climbed down to see what it was. A long slender creature with short legs and a tail half as long as its body, crept out from under the bush below her, sniffing the ground.

"ONO, Stop it! You scared me. I have never heard you make such an awful sound." Ono let out a few squeaks and slunk back. "Aww, come here, boy, I'm sorry. You were looking for me, weren't you? I believe I got lost. Do you remember the way home, Ono?" she asked.

He kept looking at her with his small eyes, wagging his tail. "No? Oh, come on, your little nose can track anything. My head hurts so bad. Help me look for anything that might help me remember how I got here so we can trace the way back home."

She began looking for footprints or any sign of her walking in the area but saw none. She threw her hands in the air and yelled, "Nothing, I see nothing!"

She looked up and saw some claw marks high up on a tree. "Wait, what's that?" she said climbing up. Reaching the marks, she placed her hand in them. It was a perfect fit. "Look Ono, I must have made these!"

She looked around and saw more claw marks. The tree branches were big and reached out far. She placed Ono on her shoulder and began jumping from tree to tree following the marks.

She was getting tired and hungry by the time the sun was at its highest. She climbed down to the ground and began looking around for berries to eat. Ono jumped off her shoulder and sniffed around. He found some plants with tall flat stems and began digging until he uncovered the roots. "Good boy, Ono. This should last us through the day."

She pulled out her water bag and washed the plants. Then she used her knife to peel the skin and cut the plant into smaller pieces. She picked two large leaves from the tree she was under, divided the pieces and berries between the leaves and sat with her legs crossed. She placed one leaf on her lap for Ono and they began to eat. A cool breeze had started moving the trees in what felt like a slow dance. She felt relaxed, but she knew she could not stay and rest for long.

"Ono, we need to keep going. Are you ready?" she asked. Ono chirped and ran up onto her shoulder. She climbed back up into a tree and began jumping through the branches.

They kept going until she came across a wooden post next to a trail. "These look like directions. Let's see, Elkwood is that way, Maplehaven is that way…" She paused and then shouted, "Oakheart!

That's my village. It's going to us take at least a day to get there. We should stop here and sleep in this tree until morning."

She chose a higher branch, found a comfortable spot, and lay down, placing Ono in her arms, and looked up. The stars were coming out, and the two moons were beginning to rise. It was peaceful and calm, she began humming a song to Ono whose eyes grew heavy and he fell asleep with a few soft whimpers. Her eyes close shortly after.

A loud crashing sound woke her up with such a jolt, almost making her fall off the branch she was sleeping on. "What was that?!" she exclaimed. "Are you ok, Ono?" She placed him on her shoulder and made her way quietly towards the sound.

A tall, bulky man was chopping trees. He had long brown hair tied in the back and a long greying beard. His axe stopped mid-swing, he sniffed the air, and then bellowed in a gruff and deep voice, "Who's there? Come out now. I know you are there. Do it quickly and I might not eat you."

The young girl jumped down out of the tree keeping distance between them and asked boldly, "Why are you cutting down the forest?"

"I need firewood. The nights are getting longer and colder," replied the man. "Who are you? Where are you from?"

"You first!" she demanded.

"I am Kovack. These are my woods, my home. Why are you here?"

"I was exploring and got lost. I think I fell and hit my head and now I don't remember who I am. I am going to Oakheart, my home, and there I will find the answer."

"Oakheart Huh? It's a long way off, and you and your little critter seem hungry. Come, sit down, and eat."

"I can find my own food," she replied.

Kovack growled, "Why look for what has already been found? He turned and walked a short way to a clearing where he had made a camp. She followed him cautiously. Kovack pointed to a log and said, "Now sit."

She sat on the log as Kovack started a fire over which an old metal pot filled with roots and berries was hanging low. He crumbled something in his palm and added it to the pot. She watched him prepare the stew, stirring it occasionally.

"What did you add to the pot?"

"Spices to bring out the flavor."

"You live here alone?"

"Yes."

"For how long?"

"For many, many long years now. Too many to remember," Kovack sighed.

"Why?"

"I don't remember, it's been too long, now here. Can't talk while you eat," Kovack mumbled as he sat opposite her on a rock. "Why do you travel so far from home? Why do you have a critter that's shaking? Why, why, why?" Kovack shook his head. "Sometimes it's better to listen. The answers will come. Use your long pointy ears, that's what they are for. You have two ears and only one mouth, you should listen twice as much as you talk." He paused for a moment. "These woods are mine. I care for them, watch them grow and cut down the old and dying. I keep it all good. I need no one."

She ate the stew in silence. Until she remembered the rumors of the trees talking and the curiosity got the better of her. "Can you talk to the trees?" she blurted out.

He looked up, paused for a moment, and said, "Yes, they speak to me."

She lit up with excitement. "What do they say!?"

"All things can be learned by listening. Go and listen."

She jumped up and ran to the nearest tree pressing her ear against it.

Kovack laughed. "Little one, you don't need to listen that hard." He stood up and slowly made his way to the tree and placed his hand on it. She did the same. He closed his eyes, took a deep breath, and said, "Eee-sa. That is your name. The trees know many things, Isa."

Isa stared in amazement. "Yes, I remember! I am Isa of Oakheart. And you are my new friend, Kovack of the Forest."

"I need no friends. You may finish your stew and continue your journey. People are waiting for you."

People, who? thought Isa.

Kovack raised his voice, "You have one mouth, you use it too much. You should listen to all around you. There is so much to learn."

I better eat fast, Isa thought. She finished her stew and said, "Thank you, Kovack. I will listen more as I go."

"Kovack hopes so," he replied, "now go and do not bother Kovack any longer."

Isa made her way down the trail. "Can you hear anything, Ono? Me either, maybe they have nothing to say to us yet," she said sighing. "We should pick up the pace and listen to the trees later. Let's go home."

The sun was setting as Isa and Ono reached Oakheart. The village was deserted. A pot of water hung over a dying fire. Baskets had been knocked over and their contents spilled onto the ground.

"Where is everyone?" Isa said loudly as she walked around, calling out. She looked up at the walkways and the huts that were built on the largest tree branches with the smaller branches weaved to form their walls.

Isa climbed up the tree checking hut after hut until she reached one near the edge of the village that felt familiar. It had to be hers. She went in and called quietly, "Hello? Is anyone here?"

No one answered.

The walls were decorated with simple drawings of the inhabitants so familiar. Her memories came rushing back and she cried out, "Oh, my sister!! and Granny!! Where is everyone?! What happened here? I only left three days ago!" Isa began sobbing as she walked to the center of the hut and placed her hands on the tree. "Please help me. Tell me what happened. Please." Tears flowed down her cheeks. Her ears twitched as she concentrated. Isa thought she could feel the trees sadness but heard nothing.

"If I can't hear the trees, maybe they can hear me," Isa said in a trembling voice. "Kovack, help me!!" Isa yelled, fell onto the floor, and cried until she had no tears left and fell asleep in the middle of the room.

2

Dark Woods

A familiar smell of roots and berries made her jump on her feet and peered out the door. Kovack was cooking on the pot she had seen the day before.

"Come down little one, Kovack heard you. I am here to help. First, we eat, then we find your family." Isa ran over and hugged him. Kovack put an arm around her, looked down and said, "We will find them, don't you worry."

"Have the trees said anything to you?"

"The trees are frightened, they said that big beasts come through yesterday. But it's ok, Kovack can track."

"I can too!!" said Isa sternly, "they ARE my family!"

"Isa, you are brave, but still young. We can find them. Be smart and use your head. We will begin after you finish eating."

She sat reluctantly and started eating quickly. "Hurry Ono, eat fast so we can go." Ono let out a few squeaks and ate his food.

After they finished eating, Kovack said, "Now grab some supplies and let's begin. The trees have said to go this way." He began walking towards the Dark Woods. "The Dark Woods are up ahead. The trees there do not speak and are not friendly. We will need to be careful."

"Can't you walk faster Kovack? We need to hurry!" Isa exclaimed.

"Do not rush Kovack, we will get there. We are two, they are many and will be much slower than us."

They walked all day until Kovack stopped them. "We will camp here where it is still safe before entering The Dark Woods."

"We must keep going. We need to find them!" Isa demanded.

"We need to rest now, these woods are dangerous, we will catch up tomorrow. We make no fire tonight so they will not see it." Kovack gave some fruit to Isa and laid down to sleep.

Isa closed her eyes and waited until she heard him snore and then crept out of camp.

Only one moon had risen, but it was enough to see. I'll find them myself she decided. She climbed up a tree and started jumping from tree to tree without noticing a shadow following her. She felt a sharp pain in her shoulder and fell to the ground. What hit her? Then she saw the shadow swooping down with wings spread wide and talons open. It was right on top of her. She screamed just as Kovack's club hit the bird, knocking it across the forest floor.

Kovack bellowed, "Kovack said rest! These woods are dangerous. You don't like to listen. The Dark Bird almost got you!" He paused, then asked softly, "Are you hurt?"

"My shoulder is hurting, but it's not bleeding."

"You're lucky Kovack saw you sneak away. Now let's get back to camp before more of those birds come. You are slower with your injury, get rest, we WILL find your family." Isa walked back to camp dragging her feet.

The light was barely making its way across the sky when Kovack woke Isa up.

"We will move now while everything in these woods is still asleep. Hurry!" Kovack insisted.

Isa jumped up and winced in pain. She had forgotten about her injured shoulder but was determined not let that slow her down. They began making their way through the Dark Woods. The trees had black bark and the leaves were a dark green. They looked scary, uninviting, and almost sad.

"The trees here do not talk, nor sing," Kovack said quietly. "We have no help but ourselves here. Stay alert."

The trees became thicker as they walked further ahead. Isa heard a noise and jumped. Kovack moved his finger to his lips quickly to silence her. Two massive creatures were asleep in a clearing up ahead. One was twitching its hind leg as if dreaming.

"Quiet now, we go around," said Kovack in a low voice, but before he finished, Ono jumped from Isa's shoulder and ran into the clearing.

"Ono, come back!!" Isa called out as he ran into the clearing and jumped up onto the beasts' legs, waking them.

They had awful yellow eyes and a long pointy snout. Their ears came to a point with tufts of hair. The beasts stood as tall as Isa and had long grey fur with white paws almost as large as Isa's chest. They growled and snapped at Ono who kept darting around their legs making them jump around trying to catch him. Kovack walked into the clearing and started laughing at the sight.

Isa looked at Kovack and pleaded, "Save him, please!"

Kovack charged towards the beasts still distracted by Ono. He grabbed them by the back of their necks and forced them to the ground. "Listen carefully, you both, Kovack needs help. You help or you run off." The grip of his hands held them firmly on the ground until they stopped struggling. He released them and said, "Make your choice!"

One of the beasts turned and lunged at Kovack, who swung his club and knocked the beast into a tree across the clearing. The beast got up, looked over at its companion and ran off into the woods. The other beast crawled up to Kovack's feet. Kovack knelt, placed his hand on its head and said, "I shall call you Kofang."

They started making their way through the forest. The trees were thick and dense, and it was getting harder to make their way through. Isa climbed up and started jumping through the trees scouting ahead. Kovack used his axe to create a path while Kofang trailed behind him. By midday, they came to a cliff. Kovack walked to the edge.

"It's too steep to climb down," he said.

"Look! I see smoke, it must be a campfire," Isa said as she pointed to smoke rising above the trees off in the distance. "It must be them!"

At that moment, the cliff gave way and began crumbling down to the forest below. Kofang leapt over and caught Isa as she fell and made his way down the cliff jumping back and forth with amazing speed. Kovack lunged his axe into the dirt to slow his fall as the ground collapsed. Kofang was the first to land safely at the bottom. Kovack pushed hard off the side and landed on his feet with a thud.

"Is everyone ok?" he asked.

"I am ok, but where's Ono?" Isa asked as she jumped off Kofang's back and started searching. Kofang began sniffing the air and walked toward Kovack. He let out a bark as he pointed his nose towards Ono, who was clinging on Kovack's back.

"How did you get on Kovack's back?" Kovack asked Ono. Ono jumped to the ground and made his way towards Kofang with his hair on his back raised.

"If you two fight, you deal with Kovack!" Kovack thundered. "You need to get past your differences!" Both looked at Kovack and then at each other and lowered their heads.

"Good, no fighting. We are all friends now."

Isa walked over and picked up Ono. "When will you learn you're not a great scary beast. You're my cute little best friend." Ono let out a few loud chirps and Isa laughed. "Yes, my cute little scary beast," she said and hugged him tight. "Can you track our family now, Ono? We can no longer see the smoke through the trees, but they should not be that far away."

Ono jumped out of her arms excited and darted off. "Ono, slow down!" she yelled, but Ono kept running and they had to chase after him.

They ran for what seemed like hours until Ono stopped and began running in circles. Isa picked him up." Good boy. You found them?" Ono squeaked excitedly. "It's ok," she said, "we'll save them."

Kovack walked ahead and investigated the camp. "They left here not long ago and can't be far ahead now. Looks like a small group. How many in your village?" Kovack asked Isa while looking at the footprints on the ground. "I count only one prisoner."

"Where are the rest?" Isa asked. "Never mind, we can ask them ourselves soon. Let's go!" Isa rushed down the trail toward her family's captors. Kofang ran ahead and blocked her way.

"Good job, Kofang," Kovack hollered as he walked fast to catch up.

Kovack glared at Isa. "Have you learned nothing? The trees spoke of Beasts that took your family. Who are they? Where are they going? Why take your family? You rush in without knowing anything. In the camp, they left many clues. There were six very large and strong beasts, and a smaller one. Seven in all. We need to be careful and NOT rush in. Last time you rushed, you got hurt. Use that thing between your ears! We track close behind and wait till they camp next. Listen and be smart."

"I am tired of waiting! What if they eat my family!" retorted Isa.

"I saw food scraps at the camp. They will not eat your family. We wait to save them tonight. Now, climb high in the trees, keep quiet and don't get too close. Kofang will go with me. Ono, if you make a noise, you go in my bag." Ono chirped twice. Kovack and Kofang walked quietly down the trail as Isa jumped from tree to tree looking for signs of her family. The sky grew darker, and she spotted smoke from a campfire up ahead.

Isa made her way back through the trees to Kovack who was not far from her and jumped down to the ground in front of him. "They have stopped not far ahead."

Kovack spoke in a low voice, "Isa, be very quiet and check out the camp. We will wait here."

The sky was fully dark by the time Isa came back. She jumped down out of the trees and walked over to Kovack.

"What did you see?" asked Kovack.

"There are five huts in the camp, one is larger than the others. There were six large beasts I could see. They look strong but after observing them for a while, they do not seem that smart. They had set up a firepit and were preparing an animal to cook over it. I did not see my family, but they could be in the huts."

"Those are not huts, they are called Yurts. They are mobile and used for traveling or camping. Kovack explained, they must be intelligent if they are setting up camp this way." Kovack stroked his beard, looked up at the night sky and then turned back to the others. "Alright, this is what we are gonna do. Kofang, run into the camp and grab the animal from over the fire, and get them to chase after you out of the camp. Isa, as soon as they leave, you and Ono search the yurts and find your family. I will take care of the remaining beasts. The moons will rise shortly, we must go now."

Kofang ran into the camp and grabbed the meat, knocked over the pans and supplies, and then darted down the trail. Four of the beasts ran after him while the other two stayed guarding two of the yurts.

Isa dashed up to them and demanded, "Where's my family!?" The beasts looked at each other confused, and then turned and reached for Isa with their huge hands. Isa darted between the legs of one of them, crawled up its back, then jumped out the way just as the second beast's fist came down hard knocking out its companion. He gasped at what he had just done, roared angrily, and lunged at Isa.

Kovack grabbed the guard from behind and knocked him out with his club. "Hurry Isa, check the yurts. I'll hide these Beasts."

Isa began searching. Ono ran to the door of one of them and stopped. He began to howl, stopping after remembering Kovack's warning and instead whimpered loudly. Isa ran over towards Ono and entered the yurt. Though dark inside, something felt familiar, and she called out, "Granny, Gesa, are you there?"

A gentle voice came from across the room, "Isa, is that you?"

Isa ran over and hugged her granny. "Granny, Are you ok? Did they hurt you?"

"Calm down, little one, they did not."

"Where's my sister?"

"She went out exploring just the same as you and was not in the village when the Tobu arrived. The prince came to ask me to return with him to their kingdom and heal his father who is extremely sick."

Kovack entered the tent quickly. "We must hurry, the other beasts will be back soon!"

"Hello, Kovack," said Granny calmly.

"Hello, Ynas," Kovack replied.

"What, you know each other!?" exclaimed Isa.

"Yes, but that's a story for another time," said Granny as she turned to Kovack. "These Tobu have asked for my help, and they are not dangerous. Please do not hurt them."

They heard Kofang howl outside the tent and Kovack hurried out to meet him. "Calm down Kofang, these beasts mean us no harm."

A Tobu warrior in purple and gold robes came out of the larger Yurt. "We are warriors, not beasts and are not here to harm anyone. I am Razak, prince of the Tobu and sole heir of King Beyla." He paused and looked over at Kofang. "But your companion does owe us a meal." Razak saw his guards charging back into the camp, he raised his hand and called out. They stopped and stood in attention. "Clean up this camp and prepare another meal over the fire."

Kofang ran into the forest as soon as the Tobu warriors started setting up the fire. He returned shortly holding a large creature in his mouth and laid it at Razak's feet.

"Thank you, Kofang," Razak said, "you are also a skilled hunter." He then looked over at Isa and said, "And you, young one, are very brave but perhaps a bit too rash. Those warriors could have really hurt you."

"You stormed through my village, took my family, left a mess, and now everyone is gone!" Isa exclaimed.

Razak explained, "We may seem scary when you first see us. That's why your friends ran when we entered your village. Many things were knocked over in the confusion that followed. We only wanted to speak with your healer. My father requested your Granny. She is our guest."

"Why do you travel with so many warriors? It's no surprise everyone ran away when you entered my village."

"It was by my father's command, it is my first time being so far away from my Kingdom. Since he became ill, he worries even more of my safety."

He turned toward Kovack, "I have heard many stories from my father of a great warrior by the name Kovack. Are you the same Kovack from these stories?" Kovack nodded. "You are well known in our Kingdom. Will the three of you join us to see my father?"

"Four!" Isa interrupted as Ono jumped up on her shoulder. "Ono and I go wherever my Granny goes!"

"I will join your group," said Kovack reluctantly.

"And what about you, Kofang?" asked Razak.

Kofang let out a low howl.

"I believe that is a yes," said Kovack.

"What about my sister?" asked Isa.

"She planned on exploring for several days and may be back in the village by now. I left a letter in the Village chiefs hut explaining everything," said Granny.

"I saw no letter when I was there."

"Did you check the Chief's hut?"

"No," Isa sighed, "I was too concerned with what might have happened to you and Gesa."

"The Chief will find the letter when they return and will explain everything."

3

The Tobu

The Tobu Chef finished cooking the meat and took platters of food in the largest Yurt.

"Join us for dinner, please. All except Kofang, who already ate," Razak said as he threw a glance at Kofang, who looked away.

"Kovack, Granny and I do not eat meat," Isa said.

"There are plenty of roots, berries, and veggies for the four of you," Razak responded.

Ono jumped off Isa's shoulder and ran into the Yurt. The others followed. Six massive Tobu were seated around a large round table full of food. Isa noticed the Tobu were gentle despite their intimidating appearance. One of them handed her a plate of food and then sat a plate of berries on the table for Ono.

Isa bowed her head and said, "Thank you." The Tobu bowed her head and continued setting plates around the table. Each bowing their head in turn as their plate was set.

Razak lowered his head and began to pray, "Great Creator, we give thanks for the animal that gave its life so we may eat and for the wild plants and roots that grow for our nourishment." He raised a cup and looked at Isa. "May you enjoy our meal and our company."

They talked of stories from times past and of faraway lands. Isa grew more curious with each story and after dinner, when she joined her granny in her tent, she asked, "Granny, the Tobu are nothing like they seem. They speak of trading with many other tribes from of faraway lands. How many tribes are there? How far does the land go? Why do we not trade or meet with these tribes?"

"Perhaps it is time to learn these things. Calm your mind little one, Listen and learn, do not be so quick to judge others by their appearance, but by their heart. It can be difficult to tell what others intentions are, so be cautious, but respectful always. Many hold other beliefs and customs. You do not need to agree with these but allow them their ways and you hold to yours. Be always willing to learn. I do, even at my age."

"Razak said a prayer out loud at dinner. We do it silently, is that part of what you mean?"

Ynas answered, "Yes, little one, each tribe has their own customs. None can be said to be wrong, simply different. Now go to sleep, tomorrow we have a long way to travel."

"Alright Granny, goodnight." But she was too excited to sleep. She played with Ono until both moons had set and finally got to sleep about the time Kovack was getting up. He checked out the camp in the early morning light. He was uneasy with the idea of traveling back with Razak. He preferred his solitude.

Razak stepped out of his tent and walked over to Kovack. "You're up this early too? I love the early morning air, and the peace and quiet." Kovack did not respond. "Kovack, your old friend would like to see you again. No one knew where you disappeared to. You are a hero to many."

"I am not a hero anymore, but I will go to watch over Isa."

"Very well, I will be happy to have you along either way." Razak turned and called out a command to his guards, who started folding up the camp and stacked everything on the table that had been used for dinner the night before. Two of the Tobu began carrying it down the trail while the others cleared out the fire pit, leaving little trace they had ever been there. Isa was impressed with how efficiently they worked. She strolled over to where Kovack and Kofang were standing.

"Thank you for helping me find my Granny. Will you tell me how you know Granny, please?"

"That was a long time ago, I am simply Kovack of the forest now," Kovack replied and turned and walked down the trail.

Isa sighed, "Ok, another day, maybe." She looked over at where Ono was playing. "Ono! Let's go." Ono climbed up on her shoulder, and Isa walked behind Kovack. Kofang dashed into the forest to hunt.

Isa's mind raced with what awaits her. She had never been this far from the village but had always wanted to know what lies beyond the trees where the moons set. Ono began humming as they walked, and Isa joined in. Isa did not remember a time without Ono. He was always there to comfort her. She asked, "How long till we reach the Tobu Village? But no one answered so she said louder. "How long till we reach the Tobu village."

"Many days, until the two moons are full, then we reach the Tobu Kingdom," Kovack said reluctantly.

"Kingdom? What is that?" asked Isa.

"You will see soon enough," Kovack sighed.

Isa kept asking many more questions as the days passed. The Tobu warriors were quiet and grunted a lot but answered some of her questions. Granny answered some, but Kovack avoided all her questions.

Isa tried getting close enough to ask Razak questions, but the guards rarely allowed it. He was kind and answered her questions when she did get close to him. Most of the answers she received were simply wait and see, but Isa was too excited to wait.

She woke late one night and saw the two moons high in the night sky. She jumped up and woke Kovack. "Kovack, the two moons are full. Are we there yet?"

Kovack sat up. "We will be there tomorrow, lil one. Best to be well rested."

"I cannot rest now! Not now! This trip has taken forever!"

"You are always in a hurry, little Isa." Kovack laughed. "Slow down, it will still be there tomorrow."

"Stop calling me little," Isa demanded, "I am almost grown!"

"You will always be little to me, now rest, or at least try," Kovack said as he turned over and went back to sleep.

Isa climbed a tree and stared at the moons till her eyes grew heavy. Ono climbed down into her lap, and they fell asleep.

The Tobu's movement packing up the camp woke Isa up. She took a deep breath, then jumped down out of the tree and walked over to everyone.

Kovack looked over at her and asked, "Are you ready?"

Isa smiled and nodded.

Kovack had a puzzled look on his face. "What, no questions?!"

Isa sighed. "I have asked so many already, it is time to wait and see."

Kovack smiled and nodded. "Very wise, little one."

Granny walked over and put her hand on Isa's head. She closed her eyes and mumbled a short blessing. She opened her eyes and looked down at Isa. "With what is to come, you will grow up so much in a short time. I believe you are ready. Walk up front with me."

They walked a few hours, talking the whole way until the trail led to a huge wall with a gate taller than the trees. Isa's eyes grew wide. One of the Tobu pulled out a beautiful gold horn and blew hard. Inside the city, Isa heard horns responding until the sound echoed throughout the city and the huge doors opened slowly. Many Tobu rushed out and crowded the trail each side of the small group of travelers. Isa heard them talking low, looking at them in amazement. One young girl stepped forward and grabbed Isa's hair. Isa pulled back, startled.

"Granny, why are they all staring?"

"They have never seen anyone like you before. No one here has red hair. You are also very small compared to them."

"I see that. But you said being different is special."

"It is, and maybe soon you will understand how special you are."

"I am not special. I am just Isa, nothing more."

Ynas laughed. "Nothing more? Soon you will see being 'Just Isa' is enough."

Kovack and Kofang walked behind Isa. The Tobu stared at Kofang who started to growl.

"Easy friend, you will need to get used to crowds now," Kovack sighed, "Kovack too."

Behind them, the crowds began cheering. Razak was walking behind two of his guards followed by the remaining guards carrying the camping supplies. Razak was waving to the crowd and calling out to them.

After entering through the great gate, they ascended a large stairway into a huge building. Isa had never dreamt of such a place. Pillars of polished stone lined the courtyard. Stairs ascended on either side of the courtyard with a large water fountain in the center. The doorway to the building was twice as tall as any Tobu. How big could they get? Isa wondered. The floors had many colors and were very shiny. Tobu guards lined each side of the long hallway. Razak called out instructions to the last four guards, who then carried the supplies off to another building. He walked to the end of the hall and stopped.

"This is the Palace of the Tobu. I will speak with my father. He was only expecting Ynas, please wait here." Razak entered the large doors.

Isa turned saying, "Kovack, have you been here before?"

"Yes, many years ago."

"Was it this beautiful back then?"

"Yes, The Tobu are great craftsman."

Razak returned and said, "My father would like to see his old friends, Ynas and Kovack. Isa, you may enter also, But Kofang must remain outside. My Guard will escort him to the stables and get him some food. A room will be made ready for each of you."

Kovack commanded, "Kofang stays with me in my room, he is my friend, and I will not allow him to be treated as a beast."

"As you wish." Razak instructed his guard, who grunted to Kofang then turned and walked off toward the rooms. Razak turned back to the door and pulled it open.

The group entered the next room. It was huge with stairs on each side curving up to a balcony. Razak walked up the stairs and continued down the hallway. He stopped at a door at the end of the hall and turned back to the others. "Please be quiet, my father is awake but very sick." He pushed the door open.

The dimly lit room had a musty odor. The curtains were closed and with what little light made it through, Isa could make out a huge bed with stone pillars at each of the four corners and purple silk draped between them.

Kovack walked over to the window and drew back the curtains. "Get up old friend, a dark room is no place for a warrior king!"

The light shown over the room, Isa was amazed at the ornate vases sitting on beautiful hand carved wood furniture.

"What are you doing!" Razak exclaimed.

The king began to laugh. "It's ok Razak. Hello, my old friend, it has been a long time. I am not a warrior anymore, just an old king."

Ynas walked over to the side of the bed. "Hello Beyla, I am happy to see your still in good spirits."

"I am, I've had great friends and a great life. And could not ask for a better son."

"You asked for me, why?"

"I wanted to see my old friend, but I never expected Kovack to be here too. What a great surprise! We can talk of the old days."

Ynas laughed. "Yes, we can, but first, let me look you over. You are sick."

"I am just getting old. Nothing to worry about," Beyla responded.

"Nonsense, I can see in your eyes. They used to be so clear. I will gather my herbs at the market."

Razak stepped forward and said, "Give me a list. I will gather them for you."

"It is best if I do it myself," Ynas replied, "Isa can join me."

Beyla looked over at Isa. "Ah yes, your daughter's daughter. Isa, come over here young one. Let me see you."

Isa walked over to the side of the king's bed, bowed, and said, "Hello King Beyla, your kingdom is magnificent. I have never seen anything like it."

"Thank you, but a kingdom is made up of the people in it, not the buildings," Beyla said. "I have been fortunate to be surrounded by great people with great skills who can build beautiful things. You have great friends too, I see. Would you like to see more of this city?"

"I would, thank you."

Beyla turned to Ynas. "You have raised her well. Go and get your herbs and return tonight. Razak, make sure they get our best rooms. Kovack, please return alone after you get settled in your room so we may speak. We have much to discuss, old friend."

Ono jumped from Isa's shoulder onto the King's bed and sniffed around.

Beyla laughed. "And who is this?"

"He has been my best friend since I was young," Isa answered.

Beyla looked down at Ono. "Hello, little friend." He reached his hand to pet Ono just behind his ear. Ono leaned into the Kings hand falling over. He rolled over and rubbed around in the covers and then climbed back onto Isa's shoulder, hiding in her hair.

Isa bowed. "I am sorry King Beyla. He is as curious as I am."

"It can be good to be curious but be careful, not everyone can be trusted. Even in my Kingdom."

Isa stood back upright. "I will be careful. Thank you for the advice."

Isa, Ynas, and Kovack left the room and waited outside for Razak. After a few words with his father, Razak joined the others in the hall.

"I am glad you all came," Razak said quietly, "I have not seen my father in such good spirits. I will take you to your rooms now."

He led the group back across the center room, passed the stairs and down to the end of the hall. He turned toward them as he pointed. "You may have these rooms across from each other."

Kovack looked into the rooms. "Where is Kofang?

"Kofang had been taken to your original quarters," Razak answered. "I will have him brought back here now that the King insisted you stay here instead."

Kovack entered his room and began unpacking.

Ynas and Isa took the room facing the rear of the palace. Ynas set her things on the bed. "We need to get to the market soon. We can unpack later. The king is sicker than he lets on."

Isa dropped her stuff in the room and got ready to go. They walked down the stairs and passed the fountain into the marketplace. Granny spent hours searching through the vendors for the herbs she wanted. Isa was more interested in all the other things for sale. Before she knew it, she had become separated from her granny.

Isa heard some howling off in the distance. "Ono, we know that howling. It's Kofang! Let's hurry!" Isa ran as fast as she could toward the howling, darting down street after street until she came to a large round building. Inside was a crowd cheering. Isa climbed the stairs to the entrance and made her way past the spectators. She grabbed the railing and looked down into the arena pit. Two large Tobu warriors were forcing Kofang to fight. He was stepping back and growling as they jabbed at him with clubs.

Isa yelled out to him, "Kofang, I'm here!" She looked around thinking hard, then ran to the rear of the seating, turned around and ran as fast as she could. She stepped up on a seat, then the rail and jumped down into the pit, calling out to Kofang. Kofang looked up and saw Isa high in the air. He ran over, leaped, and caught her before she hit the ground. The two landed and slid to a stop, spinning to face the Tobu.

"I'm here for you Kofang! Let's show these two what we can do!" Isa yelled. "Run towards them as fast as you can!"

Kofang sprang forward with amazing speed. Isa jumped off just as Kofang landed all four paws straight into the Tobu's chest, knocking him across the arena. Isa landed on the other Tobu's shoulders. Ono jumped down and ran around the Tobu warriors neck biting his ear. Isa twisted his helmet covering his eyes. The Tobu dropped his club and reached frantically for the young warrior on his back. Isa slid down his back and hit the back of his leg hard at his knee with her elbow. The Tobu warrior fell to the ground. The crowd cheered louder.

Kofang grabbed one of the clubs in his mouth and with another leap, knocked out the Tobu he was facing. He ran over to the other Tobu and stepped on his chest and as the warrior straightened his helmet, he was looking directly into Kofang's eyes and seeing his great snarling teeth, he immediately surrendered. The cheering grew so loud it was almost deafening. Ono climbed up onto Isa's shoulder. Isa patted his head, making sure Ono was ok then walked over to Kofang.

"Are you ok?" Kofang nodded and they turned and walked up toward the pit entrance.

Isa yelled to the crowd, "Is this how you treat guests in your city?!"

"What an amazing fight!" called out the announcer. "Let's hear it for the Red-haired warrior and the Grey-Haired Beast!!"

"I AM ISA OF OAKHEART! THIS IS KOFANG OF DARKWOODS! You WILL open the door and let us out of here NOW!"

The doors began to open as the cheers continued.

The announcer called out, "All hail Isa of Oakheart and Kofang of Darkwoods!" The crowd chanted as Isa left the pit.

Isa walked out of the pit and down a long dark corridor with cages on each side. An older Tobu approached her.

"That was a great battle, Isa. I am Gaf. We do not get many foreigners anymore. Will you return for another battle?"

Isa glared at Gaf. "We are not here to fight. And I don't appreciate you trapping Kofang and forcing him to fight."

Gaf raised his hand to his chin. "My mistake, I know of these great beasts. The Draufganger are friends to no one. I didn't know he was your friend."

Isa scowled. "He IS my friend, and no one will force him to do anything."

"Understood, great warrior." As Gaf bowed, Isa walked past him and out of the arena.

"We need to find our way back to the market, Kofang. I lost Granny there. She is probably worried. You did do great in there though, and you too, Ono."

Ono squeaked and Kofang let out a little growl. They walked back to the market, getting lost a few times along the way. They couldn't help but notice the Tobu all staring and whispering as they walked by.

When they finally found the market, Granny was no longer there, and Isa decided to go back to the palace rooms. They found Kovack in his room and began to tell him what happened.

"I heard," Kovack replied, "rumors of a great Red-hair warrior have already reached the Palace. I heard the crowd from here. It seems you did well. And well done for helping Kofang."

Isa looked confused. "You heard, and you didn't help? I could have been hurt."

Kovack chuckled. "Yes, you could have, but that has never stopped you before. Kovack heard the crowd but did not know it was Isa."

Kofang walked up to Isa and rubbed his head up against her, then walked over to a corner of the room and laid down for a rest.

Isa watched Kofang then looked up at Kovack. "Why did they do this? Gaf told me he never seen a beast like Kofang be a friend to anyone."

Kovack answered, "Maybe no one tried before, Kofang is our friend. Kovack will speak with Razak. Gaf always tries to make exciting battles."

Isa looked puzzled. "You know Gaf too? What more are you not telling me. And where is Granny?"

Kovack looked away. "Too many questions, Ynas is with Beyla. It was twenty summers ago. Kovack was here. Many ways have not changed, some have. They still like battles. Anyone can fight."

"Have you fought here?"

"Many times."

Isa looked at Kovack and wondered who he really was but decided to go find Granny and save her questions for later. As she started out the door, Kovack stopped her.

"Best to get sleep, leave your granny to her work."

Isa looked into his eyes and saw sadness and wondered what happened. "Ok, I'll get some sleep, but I want answers tomorrow."

Kovack remained silent as she walked out of the room.

It was not easy to sleep at first with all the thoughts racing through her mind. But she was exhausted, and she was asleep before long. With the curtains covering the windows, Isa slept till the sun was high in the sky. A loud knock at the door woke her. Ono jumped at the sound. Isa opened the door to find a young Tobu girl standing there holding a plate of food. She opened the door farther and motioned for her to enter. The young girl entered and set the plate down on the table, turned and looked at Isa, smiled and quickly left the room. Isa looked at Ono, shrugged and went over to the food to eat. Ono jumped down and waited for Isa to set a plate for him. They ate till they were full. Isa changed into fresh clothes and walked down the hall looking for Granny.

She knocked on King Beyla's door lightly. Granny opened the door just a little.

"Hello lsa, the King needs rest. I must stay with him for a while. Please go explore the city with Kovack until I call for you." Ynas gave a stern look to Isa. "And I prefer you stay away from the arena."

"You heard?" Isa said as she looked down.

"Yes, everyone has, and I am proud of you, but do not return there."

Isa nodded and headed toward Kovack's room. When she reached the stairs, she saw many Tobu gathered in the lower level. She could just make what they were saying. Isa backed up and hid just out of view. They were discussing how the Tobu guards were defeated yesterday by a small Red-haired girl. They were to be punished for losing a prisoner to her. Isa didn't approve of what the guards had done to Kofang, but she didn't want them punished either.

She charged down the stairs.

"No one needs to be punished any more than they already have. And if anyone disagrees, they can face me themselves!" The

Tobu turned and looked at Isa in surprise just as Razak entered the room.

"Calm down!. There will be no punishment or further fighting!! Now get back to your tasks." Razak walked over to Isa. "You are very brave…or foolish. You should not challenge the Tobu."

"They were trying to put Kofang into a cage and force him to fight and I will not allow that! He is our friend!" Isa retorted.

Razak set his hand on Isa's shoulder and said, "I heard, and I do apologize. He was grabbed while he ate his dinner. The Tobu enjoy testing their strength. They can get a bit rough at times. You need to be careful."

"I am scared of nothing!"

"I can see that. Please heed my words, though," Razak said softly.

Isa looked sternly at Razak, sighed, then nodded. "I will try. Do you know where Kovack is?"

"I believe he is down at the market. Do you want me to escort you?"

"It will not be necessary. I will wear this cape to cover my hair and be careful."

"Very well, but I will be listening for further commotions." Razak turned and walked away.

Isa walked out the large doors and down past the pillars. She could see the crowds of Tobu down in the market. She walked down into the crowds and began to search for Kovack.

"Knowing Kovack, we will find him at the weapon shop," she said to Ono.

Making her way through the crowd was easy for a young girl of her size. It did not take long before she found the weapon shop. She walked in and found no one inside. The biggest weapons hung on the walls, shields and staves were propped up against the walls. She stepped forward to the glass case at the counter. Inside, there were two small weapons. The blades were sharp and curved down to a point. Three rubies were embedded in the thickest area of the blade. The blade extended from one end of grip and curved back around to a point making it an extension of your fist.

An older Tobu walked up from the other side of the counter.

"Hello, Red-haired warrior," Gaf said. "Do you like those weapons? They were made for Tobu children. They may just fit your hands."

"You…?" Isa looked surprised.

Gaf continued, "I own this shop and manage the arena. They go together nicely."

"I guess so. They are beautiful, but I don't need a weapon."

"Everyone needs a weapon to defend themselves. After the incident in the arena, I will give these to you as a gift. Here, try them out. There is a training area out back."

"Thank you, Gaf." Isa put them on and walked outback.

Kovack was there trying out a new club. Kovack looked at her and asked," What are you doing here?"

"This is where you've been?" Isa asked. She showed him the weapons in her hands.

Kovack looked at her and shook his head. "Very well then, you will learn to use them now and train here with me. From watching you, I can see your granny has taught you the basics of breathing and meditation. We will continue from there. Weapons are an extension of you. See in your mind, feel in your heart. Close your eyes and find your stance. Now let's go through the movements."

Kovack began to show her how to move her hands, her feet, and her body. "These weapons fit you. You will move differently for different weapons. Practice your breathing as you move. After that you will learn where to hit enemies to stop them without injuring them badly. There are points on a body that can immobilize a person."

Isa practiced for hours every day here. Gaf made her covers for her blades so she could now practice without hurting anyone. The braided leather was soft with red gems embedded across the sides. The leather hung down at each end. Isa sparred with Kovack in fierce duels over the next few weeks. It did not take long till she had mastered using these weapons.

One evening as Isa returned to the palace, she found granny in their room. "Granny, you're finally here. How is the king?"

Ynas looked at Isa. "The king has recovered. We are to have a feast tomorrow. He has requested all our presence. You have grown up a lot these past few weeks, Isa. May I see your weapons?"

Isa pulled them out and handed them to her granny. Ynas held them into her hands. She sighed and brought them closer to her eyes. "I remember these well, my old friends."

"Your old friends?" Isa looked confused. "What do you mean?"

"We are remembered well here. I did not expect to see all this after so much time. You will learn more at the feast."

"Granny, when are you going to tell me everything? I am ready."

"Ready or not, with all that is happening, you will soon know. Now, get some sleep. No training tomorrow. I need to speak with Kovack. I will see you in the morning."

Ynas left the room quietly and knocked on the door across the hall. Kovack opened the door and invited her inside. They spoke for hours about all that happened since they had left many years ago.

The morning was filled with music and laughter. The palace was busy with preparations for the feast. For the first time in weeks, Isa walked down through the market without going straight to the weapon shop to train. She noticed the fine clothing, pottery, the fruit stands, the animals, and the many things made of leather. Isa stopped at each stand asking the vendors where they were from and how far they traveled. She learned there were four main kingdoms each surrounded by many small villages. The chiefs governed the villages and sent taxes to the king, who in turn provided security, maintained the roads, and settled disputes. Isa learned that her village was Tobu territory, but she never heard of the Tobu before they entered her village.

The Shops started to close up when the sun reached its highest point of the day, and the streets began to fill with everyone headed to the Palace courtyard.

"Oh no, I forgot about the feast, Ono. We need to hurry!" Isa ran quickly back to the palace cutting through the crowd and made her way up the courtyard stairs to the palace entry and pushed her way past the crowd to the door. She ran up the stairs and down the hall to her room. When she opened the door, Isa found that clothing had been laid out on the bed for her. She put them on quickly and fixed her hair with a twist, making a bun and placing a hand carved wooden hair stick through it, then straightened down her gown and headed out toward the main hall.

King Beyla was sitting at the center of the main table with Razak sitting on his right side and Kovack on his left. Next to Kovack was Ynas and then an empty chair. Isa walked quickly over to it, drew back the chair to sit down as Ynas looked at her and smiled. Isa had never seen her Granny looking so radiant. She wore a long white gown with an emerald sash around her waist. Emerald and silver jewelry adorned her grey hair that hung down to the floor over her chair. A matching emerald necklace hung around her neck. Isa looked at Kovack. He looked so different. His beard had been trimmed and he was wearing traditional Tobu formal attire. He had silver bracelets around his wrists and a medal pinned to his chest. The sadness was gone from his eyes.

Razak looked over at Isa and nodded for her to sit.

He stood up. "Attention, please!" He waited until the crowd settled down and continued, "for many moons now our king, my father, has been extremely ill. He sent me to bring back his dear friend, Ynas the healer who has watched over him for the past several weeks. He is well again and has joined us this day. Stand now and listen now to the words of your King."

Beyla stood up and acknowledged his son, who bowed in return. The crowd bowed with Razak. "My dear countrymen, I am most pleased to return to your company," the king began, "I thank Ynas for coming to my side. I never thought she would be accompanied by my old friend, Kovack. And joining them both is Isa, the Red-haired warrior. Many of you have met these three over the past few weeks as they toured our Palace grounds. Tonight, we honor them." Beyla raised his glass. "To our friends, may they prosper in all they do!" The crowd's cheers rose so high, you heard nothing else. "Now, to all within our great palace, please, enjoy the feast!"

The clapping and cheering continued until the music started. Everyone began eating, talking, and laughing. When most had finished eating, Razak walked over to Isa and extended his hand. Isa looked puzzled but took it and he led her in front of the table. He pulled her close and said, "Dancing is very much like fighting. Follow my lead, just don't hit me." He began with a few steps. The movements felt similar to how Kovack had trained her in the weapon shop. It did not take long before she was dancing across the floor with him.

Kovack pulled back his chair, got up and offered his hand to Ynas. She smiled and they joined the others dancing in the Palace Gardens. Both moons had risen, and the stars shone brightly as they danced and sang to the music. More couples joined them, until the gardens were full.

The sky grew light by the time the dancing had stopped. Isa bowed to Razak and excused herself to her room. Kovack escorted Ynas back to her room and then went back to his own.

Tobu city was quiet the next day. King Beyla walked around his city. He was delighted to see everyone so happy, but he knew it would not last. Let them sleep…for now.

4

A New Quest

The next morning, King Beyla asked for the four to join him in his chambers.

"Kovack, Ynas, Isa, and Kofang, though I fear you will not fully understand me. My becoming sick was by no accident. King Melor of the Goshan Kingdom has fallen and I fear the other two Kings are next or maybe even responsible. Since the Great War ended and we established the four Kingdoms, we have enjoyed peace. Although uneasy at times, we have all stayed within our borders and conducted trades and exchanged vital information. About the time I became ill, the borders were closed, and all information and trading ceased. Only villages within our border continue to trade in our city."

Isa looked up at Beyla. "Great King. war? What war?"

Kovack interrupted, "A great long war. Many lives were lost, many friends among them."

Isa resumed, "When did it end? I did not hear of any war."

Ynas answered, "The Great War took your mother, my beloved daughter. I could not bear to stay and face the hatred anymore, so I took you away to our village and kept you safe."

"What about my father?"

"I do not know, he never returned," answered Ynas.

Kovack said in a low voice, "He was fighting beside Kovack, and we got separated. Kovack tried to find him but could not. I do not know more."

Isa looked at Kovack in disbelief and yelled, "You knew my father! Why did you not say anything before?!"

"You were not ready yet," Kovack answered, "you are now."

Beyla interrupted, "Settle down, many things happened that should not have. I am asking for you to help keep them from starting again. Razak and a Tobu guard can accompany you.

Kovack looked at the King. "Razak should stay in the palace to keep peace and promote trade, we will travel to my old home and speak with Queen Shea. We can offer to help her if needed and ask her to open her borders."

Ynas nodded. "I agree with Kovack. The four of us will move quicker than a large group. We will prepare and leave tomorrow."

"Very well," answered Beyla. "Take my finest hoofas. They are fast and can travel great distances."

Kovack nodded and turned toward the door, holding it open for the other three to walk out. He glanced at King Beyla, then turned, walked out of the room, and slowly shut the door.

They returned to their rooms and began preparations to leave. There was a knock on Isa's door. She walked over and opened it. Razak was standing there holding something in his hands. He reached out and handed them to Isa.

"I had these made for you. Will you use them on your journey?" Isa reached out and took them into her hands. He continued, "They are made from the strongest metal in the kingdom. They will slide over your fingers and when you make a fist, any enemy will feel it. I can see into your heart. You do not wish to hurt people. Use these if you need to protect yourself. The rubies embedded will add to your power when you concentrate and learn to use them."

"Thank you, Razak. I will use them only if I must."

Razak nodded, said goodnight turned and left.

Isa closed the door and walked over to her granny. "Granny, tell me about these gems, please. How do they help?"

"The gems respond to your inner strength and increase your abilities. You train and find the gem that syncs with you. You have been training for so long. We all can see the fire that burns inside you. You are a ruby, just as I was once. Now I heal with the emerald and will fight no more. The weapons you got from the weapon shop were mine. I left them with Gaf when I lost my daughter. Everything changed that day. He was an old friend. He kept them all these years. He knew who you were when he saw you in the arena. No other tribe has red hair like us. I am glad he gave you my old weapons. I do not wish for you to fight, but I know it may be necessary."

"Granny, you fought in the war. You were a warrior, not a healer? You can change your gems? How?"

"Not everyone can. Usually, you lose the connection with them. My desire to heal was great after everything I saw. I am grateful the emerald allowed me the use of its power. I was a great warrior but now I am a better healer."

"Can you teach me to fight?" asked Isa quietly.

"No, I have lost that desire and ability completely. A fighter without desire is no fighter at all. I may be able to show you the way to access your gemstone. That's up to you, really. You must empty yourself, have no emotion, no thoughts, just feel. Feel everything around you, the trees, the wind, the animals. There is an energy in everything. You must feel it."

"Is that how Kovack talks to trees?"

Ynas laughed. "Talks? Not quite. It is more of a feeling inside. Kovack can teach you much more than he gives away. He just needs to remember how to connect with his gem. Practice feeling everything around you before we continue with this discussion. I will get some rest now. Riding a Hoofa is not easy. You will need your strength for tomorrow."

Isa walked over to the window. Both moons were rising, one halfway behind the larger one. The light they provided made it easy to see across the palace and out far into the forest. A gentle breeze swept through the trees. Isa breathed deep. Feel everything, she thought. She took another deep breath. "This might take some practice." Isa walked over to her bed. Her thoughts were of the coming trip, no... adventure. So many new things. She never imagined anything like this before. What would she have done if the Tobu hadn't come to her village? She was never truly happy there. It was beautiful and peaceful, but I was missing something. Now she had more adventure than she ever dreamed of and still, something was missing. Isa closed her eyes as she said, "I will find what's missing," and fell asleep.

The morning found them busy saying goodbyes. The hoofas were ready, and the provisions had already been packed. Crowds had come to see them off. Razak escorted them to a large gate at the opposite side of the city they had entered. They all turned to Razak and bowed. Razak looked at Isa, bowed his head and turned to leave. They mounted their Hoofas and were off with a light kick to the hindquarters. Kofang had no trouble keeping pace behind them. Kovack led the group, Ynas was second followed by Isa, who had insisted she ride her own but was already believing that may have been her best idea.

The hoofas were extremely fast, and it was difficult to hold on. Isa was completely exhausted by the time the sun was at its highest. Kovack called for them to stop, but when Isa tried to stop, her hoofa darted off at full speed. Isa held on as tight as she could, yelling for help. The hoofa made a sudden turn and Isa flew through the air. She bounced, rolled, and fell down a deep hole in the ground. The roots protruding into the hole slowed her fall and she hit the ground with a thud, knocking the wind out of her. She gasped for air for a moment and looked up. The hole was so deep that no light penetrated. Kofang was the first to arrive at the hole and began digging down around the hole to make it bigger. Kovack came to a quick stop and jumped off his hoofa. He looked around, trying to find another way to get to Isa. Ynas came up last, more calmly than the other two. She stepped down from her hoofa and walked over to the hole. Ynas knelt and put her hand on the ground.

"She is all right. She is with a friend. We will go set up camp near the entrance to the cave and wait for her there," Ynas said.

Kovack looked at Ynas and could tell by the look in her eyes that he must do as she said. He put his hand on Kofang's back and pulled him back away from the hole.

"Come, Kofang, we will go for now and see Isa soon. We will go with Ynas to set up camp and wait."

Kofang whimpered. Isa's scent was strong, but he could not reach her. He turned and left with Kovack.

5

Inner Power Awakens

Isa caught her breathe and climbed to her feet. The fall had knocked the wind out of her, but she was ok. The area was dark and damp. The air was thick and moist, and she squinted in the dark to see better. She could feel an overpowering presence. Someone was there.

She asked, "Who's there?"

"It is I."

"Who is I?"

"I am only me. Who are you?"

"I am Isa of Oakheart. How do I get out of here?"

"You don't. Here is here, and here is where you stay." The voice was getting louder as she came closer.

"I cannot stay. I have people who need me."

"Why do they need you? What can you do?"

"I can help."

"Then help me."

"I do not know you, but how can I help?" Isa asked as she looked around in the dark.

"You would help me before knowing what I need?"

"Yes, first, I would like to see you though."

The area began to glow with dim light coming from gems on the cavern wall. "Is this better?"

Isa eyes opened wide with astonishment. She was in a large cavern with tunnels going out in four directions. "Where is here?"

"Here is where you are."

"That is not an answer."

"It is a correct answer."

"Come out where I can see you," Isa requested.

"Very well." A large creature stepped out from one of the tunnels.

In the dim light, Isa could make out the brown fur and large eyes. It walked on two legs and had a short tail. It was as tall as the tallest Tobu. It charged at her and caught Isa off guard. She stumbled to grab at her weapons as she rolled to the left and just missed getting hit. The beast charged at her again. Isa had her knuckles on by now and pushed off a rock, diving under its large body hitting it at the ankle as it passed. The beast howled and turned toward her again. Isa took her stance and prepared for another charge. The beast pounded the ground and knocked Isa down. He charged again. Isa rolled back and pushed up with her feet and swung as hard as she could, hitting the beast in its large nose. He lurched back, grabbed his nose with both hands and turned and disappeared down the tunnel he came out of.

"Well done, Isa." A woman entered the cavern from the opposite tunnel. "I am Acacia. The rumors I hear are true, Isa of Oakheart, the Red-haired warrior. You have skills, but not yet fully developed." Acacia was a beautiful tall lady with dark brown hair. She was thin with pale skin with green eyes. "Who was that, and why did he attack me?" Isa asked.

"That is my friend. He was testing your abilities. The fight would have lasted longer, but his nose is very sensitive."

"I am sorry I didn't want to hurt him."

"Isa, you must give all or do nothing, going halfway will get you hurt. To face what is coming, you must get a lot stronger."

"Kovack says the same thing, but I do not like to fight."

"That is admirable but cannot always be helped. You have great strength and if you use it properly, you will avoid most fighting."

"How did you light the cave?"

"I connect to my gem. Have you found your gem yet?"

"My granny says I am a Ruby, but they do not glow for me yet."

"A ruby? Hmm, I can see that in you. Who is your Granny?"

"Ynas of Oakheart."

"You are the granddaughter of the mighty Ynas?!" Acacia whistled and stepped back. The cavern began to shake. Beasts came in from the four tunnels and charged towards Isa. "All out or die, Isa of Oakheart!"

Isa looked at Acacia confused and then turned back toward the beasts. She reached for her knuckle and took her stance. She charged toward the first beast as it got close enough. She extended her hand and Ono ran down her arm and jumped onto the beast. The beast hesitated at the surprise attack. Isa took the chance and landed a hard blow to the beast's nose but got no reaction. What now!? she thought. The beast swung his arm hitting her in her side and knocked her across the cavern. She tumbled to a stop at the far wall coughing trying to catch her breath. The other beasts surrounded her.

Acacia said in a loud voice, "What now, Isa, will you give up so easily?"

Isa got to her feet, took a deep breath and cleared her mind.

"These beasts will not stop. You must stop them. Use your blades!" Acacia commanded.

Isa put her knuckles away and put on her blades. She took another deep breath and concentrated. Her chest hurt, but she charged again, darting in between the beasts spinning and slicing at each as she passed them. Grunts and growls filled the cavern. The beasts turned and charged again. Isa knew she would have to hurt them or else.

"Come Ono! All in now!"

Ono jumped from beast to beast, distracting them. while Isa darted back and forth, slicing at their legs, then arms.

Acacia yelled, "Not enough!"

Isa could feel the warmth growing in her body. She had no thoughts but stopping these beasts. She charged and, as she swung her blades, they started glowing red. She kept swinging. and the glow grew brighter. Isa was moving so fast! through the cavern, the beasts could not keep up. She darted in and out, slicing the beasts until they fell or retreated. The last beast stood before her. She glared at it, her blades glowing bright red.

The beast kneeled and bowed its head. Isa looked over at Acacia confused.

"Well done, Isa of Oakheart, the ruby accepts you." Acacia walked over to Isa. "I will heal the beasts, do not worry. Calm yourself now."

Isa's eyes grew dark, and she collapsed.

Isa awoke on a bed. Candles lit the room, but the smell was unfamiliar to her. She heard someone in the next room moving around. She tried to get up. Oh, my body is sore all over, she thought. She made her way out to the other room. She saw Acacia working at a table.

"Good, you're awake."

"How long was I out?"

"Three sunrises."

"How can you see the sun down here?

Acacia laughed. "We walk in the forests during the day. How are you feeling?"

"My whole body aches."

"My healing is not as advanced as Ynas, I did my best. Your cuts and bruises are easy, however using a gem for the first time is hard on your body. You did very well. Remember how it felt and it will get easier each time."

"Are the beasts ok?"

"Yes, they are all ok. You have greatness in you. I had to bring it out. Your friends are waiting for you. I will escort you to the surface as soon as you're ready to go."

"What happened to here is where you stay?"

"I have much respect for Ynas. You may leave now."

"I have many questions I want to ask you, but I do not wish to keep my friends waiting. I am ready."

"Very well, we can talk as we go." Acacia guided Isa down a long tunnel. Off in the distance, she could see a bright light. She looked up at Acacia. "What is your gem's ability?"

"The Amethyst promotes plant growth and closeness with nature. I can communicate with the animals as well," answered Acacia.

"I thought anybody could talk with plants and animals."

"Not quite, it takes a lot of practice for someone to understand what plants and animals feel and think. I can hear them as easily as speaking with you now."

"How can I learn how to listen? Kovack made it look easy."

"Listening is easy. Hearing is much harder. You must settle yourself. Calm your mind and really listen."

"I am calm. Everything else needs to move faster."

Acacia laughed. "You may miss many things if you move fast all the time. Pay attention to everything around you, use all your senses, and you will realize what you are missing. I will stop here. Your friends are waiting at the tunnel entrance. I enjoyed our time together, Isa. May we meet again soon." Acacia held out her hand her palm facing Isa.

"Thank you for your wisdom, Acacia." Isa placed her hand up against Acacia's hand, which began to glow purple and grew warmer. Isa concentrated, and her hand began to glow red. The colors blended where the two palms met.

"Now we are connected, call on me if you have need." Isa nodded and turned to walk away, feeling very warm inside.

The Sun was so bright she could barely see when she exited the tunnel, and it took her eyes a few moments to adjust.

Kovack was sitting on a rock. "Had quite an adventure, lil one?"

"I met a new friend, who helped me connect with my gem."

"Then it was worth waiting for you. You need to go see Kofang, he misses you."

Isa looked up at Kovack and felt something she never noticed before. Who was he really? She turned and walked over toward the camp calling for Kofang. Kofang walked out from behind the tent. Isa thought she could see a smile as he walked up to her.

"I am ok, Kofang."

Kofang lowered his head. She could feel the warmth in him as she placed her hand to his forehead.

"I missed you, my friend. Thank you for waiting for me."

Ono jumped out onto Kofang's back and curled up into his fur. Kofang jumped back and shook his whole body, sending Ono flying. Ono landed on the tent and ran down and back across the ground, charging at Kofang. Kofang stamped his feet as Ono ran around, trying to bite Kofang's legs.

"Cut it out, both of you!" Isa yelled, "you fight like you are brothers!" Kofang looked at Ono and growled. Ono's hair stood up all down his back and he walked up nose to nose with Kofang. Isa reached down and picked up Ono. "Will you ever learn? You great and terrible beast, Kofang is our friend, right Kofang?" Isa looked over at Kofang with a mean look. "You need to stop too, Kofang. No more fighting, please."

Kovack walked into the camp. "We will rest the remainder of today and leave tomorrow."

6

A Curious Youth

Isa woke up early but stayed in bed, staring up at the sky. The past few weeks were playing in her head. She looked over at her weapons and the rubies embedded in them. She had seen her granny heal before, but never saw her gem glow. There was so much to think about. Who was Kovack? Why won't he talk about his past? The world is much bigger than I imagined. I feel so humble now. They say I am special, but I don't feel that way. I am only Isa.

Ono woke up and walked up Isa's chest. He sniffed her lip and her nose.

"Stop Ono, that tickles!! How do you always know what to do to make me laugh? I am glad you are here with me. We should get up and get some food. You are hungry, aren't you?"

Ono rubbed his head on her chin then jumped off and ran over to the food storage bag. Isa got up, rolled up her sleeping pad and put it away. She walked over and opened the food storage and pulled out some berries and roots. She set up a pot and started the fire then cut up the ingredients and filled the pot. The smell of the stew filled the camp as it warmed up. Isa used a large flat rock to serve the food in five wood carved bowls. Kofang was the first to get up. Kovack and Ynas walked over to Isa and sat down.

"Smells delicious," said Ynas, "I love the smell of berries in the morning."

Kofang smelled his bowl and turned his head away. He walked out into the forest to hunt. After breakfast, they all packed up the supplies on the hoofas. Everyone was moving slowly this morning.

Kovack called out, "We are in no hurry today. After Isa's little incident, we'll take it a little slower."

"I will be okay riding the hoofa today," Isa said.

"We will see," Kovack replied.

They started down the trail with Kofang running behind. The trail narrowed down making Isa a bit nervous, but she would not let it show. The trail opened up, and they saw a small village ahead.

"Can we stop and check out the village?" Isa called out to Kovack, "I need a break."

"We can stop here for a while." Kovack pulled the reins back and slowed the Hoofa to a stop.

Ynas pulled up next to him and sighed, "I am too old for this."

"Me too," replied Kovack.

Ynas looked over at him and shook her head as she giggled. They tied their Hoofas up to a tree and walked into the village. It was still morning, and the vendors were busy setting up their shops. Isa explored the goods. There were many things she had never seen before. She stopped at a shop selling leather and wood goods in weird shapes. She looked at them with curiosity so closely she barely noticed the young kid talking to her.

"Do you like them?" he asked. "Do you like them?" he repeated a little louder.

Isa turned and looked at the young boy.

"What are they?" she asked.

"I saw them in my head and then I made them myself."

"That is impressive, but what are they?"

"They are toys, you play with them. Well...kids do, anyway. I am not a kid, so I don't."

Isa looked puzzled. "You're kinda young. I would say you're still a kid."

Fig became serious. "I have twelve cycles. I am too old for toys. I only make them. I make other stuff too. Wanna see?"

"Sure." Isa became curious. She thought this young boy had quite an imagination.

He led her to the back of the shop. As she walked around the corner, she couldn't believe her eyes. The things he had built were huge.

"What are these things?!" she exclaimed.

Fig shrugged. "I get ideas and then I build'em. These don't work like they do in my mind, but I'll keep trying."

Isa pointed to an area on the back of the thing. "Do you sit on this? And what is this called? And how does it work? And..."

The young boy stopped her. "One question at a time. First, I am called Fig. And yes, you sit there, I have not named it. There's no point till it works really, and as I said, it doesn't work. It's a work in progress. But I believe it will, or I hope it will, we'll see."

"Oh, sorry, I am Isa, nice to meet you. You are very interesting, Fig. I wonder what else you see in your mind."

"I am not interesting, I'm just Fig. Where are you from, Isa?"

"Oakheart."

"I do not know of Oakheart, where is it? I also make maps, well... I'm just assisting the map business my father started."

"Um, I am not sure really, we came through the Tobu kingdom."

Fig went into the shop and came out a few moments later holding a rolled-up canvas. He put it on the table and rolled it out. There were drawings of mountains and rivers and trees. Isa had seen something similar on a large wall in the Tobu Kingdom. She never imagined you could roll it up and take it with you.

"We can backtrack the time and the direction you traveled in and using some key points, we can locate Oakheart," Fig continued.

"You're brilliant, Fig. Did you draw these?"

"These were drawn by my father. He is better at drawing than I am. I can read them very well, though."

"Where is your father now?"

"He travels around to update his maps but has been gone for too long now." Fig looked back down at the map and continued, "So, how long did you travel from Oakheart to the Tobu Kingdom? And in which direction?"

Isa had to think hard. She was so worried about her family back then, she couldn't remember details. "Can we do this later? I want to look at more of these toys."

"Sure, we can update the map later." Fig saw the look in Isa's eyes and could tell she didn't want to talk about what happened back then. "We can do this another time. Come with me." He rolled up the map and walked with her around the front of the store. "Pick one."

"What?" Isa looked at him, confused.

"Pick one, anyone you want. Just show it to people on your journey and mention that it was made here."

Isa smiled. "Thank you, Fig. That is truly kind." Isa picked a toy and looked over at Fig who nodded. She waved at him as she turned and began to walk through the other vendors.

An odd-shaped hut on wheels was stopped in the center of the other vendors. It had a large beast harnessed at the front, eating from a wooden bucket. The sides of the hut were propped open, and glass containers of various sizes and colors lined the shelves inside. As she got closer, she could smell something brewing. Tables had been set out and villagers were sitting, drinking, and laughing.

"What will you have?" A deep voice echoed as she rounded the back of the hut. Isa jumped. The big man laughed. "Sorry, lil lady, you want a drink?"

"What kind of drinks do you have?" Isa asked.

"A lil of everything. Make your cares go away or just raise your mood a bit. Good drinks for good people. Try this brew I made from licorice roots." He handed her a mug.

Isa sipped a little. "Wow, this is really good. You make all these yourself? Where are you from? Why does your hut have wheels?"

"You ask too many questions, drink your drink." And he walked off and began talking with the other guests.

"But what are you called?" Isa called out after him.

He looked back. "I am called Eber." And then continued talking with the other guests.

Isa shrugged. The drink was good, at least. She walked further down through the vendors. She saw people from many different villages here, just like in the Tobu Kingdom. They must travel, she thought. That must be a fun way to live. Isa turned the corner and walked up to another vendor. A big guy was sitting in a chair. He had a white cloth draped up to his neck. An older man stepped out from the back of the shop with a pouch in his hand. He set it down on a small table and rolled it open revealing strange metal things inside.

She walked up and introduced herself, "Hello, I am Isa. What are you doing?"

"Hello Isa, I am Bur. I help keep people healthy. This Goshan here needs his teeth checked, his nails trimmed, and his hair cut and washed."

"Not washed," the Goshan man grunted.

Bur continued, "Well, you do. You need to keep clean. It's better for your health. Now sit still! I have a lot of work to do."

Isa watched as Bur picked up a few of the metal things and asked, "What are those?"

Bur explained, "These are my tools. I had Fig's father make them so I could work better. I hope he returns soon though. I need these sharpened."

"I met Fig, he is a curious kid."

"He is indeed, a very smart young lad. Takes after his father, maybe even smarter, and he has a great imagination. Do you want some work done or just want to watch?"

"I do not know what work I would have you do."

Bur walked around Isa. "Hmm...let me see. You look very healthy, smile."

Isa smiled showing her teeth.

"Yes, you have all your teeth," Bur said as he took her hand, "and your claws are very sharp." Bur nodded as he continued, "You do a good job taking care of yourself."

He turned to the Goshan. "You could learn a lot from this young lady."

"Hmmph." The Goshan man looked at Isa with a scowl on his face.

"No one's fault but your own," said Bur. "If you took better care of your body, you would not go through this now."

Isa smiled, she was glad now that she had listened to her granny. "It was nice to meet you Bur, I will leave you to your work."

"Ok, young lady, I am happy to have met you, too."

Isa walked out of the shop and turned back the way she came. We were only supposed to rest a little while. I should get back, she thought. Isa walked up to Eber's cart and returned the mug he had given her. "It was really good, thank you."

"I am glad you liked it and thank you for returning my mug," replied Eber.

"What else do you make?" Isa asked.

"I make elixirs from plants all over the four kingdoms. Some to heal, some to simply enjoy."

"So, you could tell me a lot about the four kingdoms?"

"I could, but I won't. Go see them for yourself. That's the best way, hearing someone's story is interesting, but cannot compare to doing it yourself. Live your own life. It has been nice chatting, but I need to prepare for mid-day meal. Many people will be coming here. Next time I see you, I want to hear of your adventures." Eber turned and climbed into his Hut.

Isa stared as he climbed. "Ok, I will go and see all four kingdoms and then come here to tell you all about it." She turned and continued toward the others a bit confused. He was different. Who doesn't like hearing stories? she thought to herself, but he is right, living it is better.

Isa heard a lot of yelling up ahead. She started running toward it. Fig was in the middle of the street, pushing one of his inventions. It had two wheels, one on each side and a seat in the middle. A group of boys were yelling and making fun of him.

Isa ran up to Fig. "Are you alright?"

"Yes, just another idea not quite working."

Isa turned to the boys. "Why are you yelling at him? You should help him!"

"Why would we help that kid, he makes stupid stuff!" the biggest kid yelled.

Isa yelled back, "Maybe in your eyes, but I see amazing things that you or I can't even imagine!"

The kid retorted, "But they don't even work. How stupid is that?"

"Stupid is sitting around doing nothing! I will help him, and you all can go back to your boring life, sit on your bottoms, and do nothing. Being mean to others is wrong!" Isa walked right up to him and stared up into his eyes. He was a whole head taller, but she didn't care. "You WILL leave my friend alone!!"

The kid glared down at Isa. "Why should we? This is part of our fun."

"Why is picking on smaller people fun?" Isa said sternly. She slid her hands onto her weapon, then pulled her hand back out, as mean as they were being, she did not want to hurt them.

The kid looked around and gestured with his hand. "There is nothing to do in this town so we will do what we want."

"Nothing to do?!" Isa grew even more furious. "It looks like Fig is doing a lot. You three could be helping him, maybe then these things he makes will work. Now THAT would be fun!"

"Isa, it's ok," Fig said quietly, "I don't even listen to them, I know who I am, so it doesn't bother me."

"It bothers me, Fig. This shouldn't happen to anyone," Isa did not move her gaze as she said, "You all need to leave. Fig is my friend, and I will not allow you to mistreat him. Go and find a new FUN activity."

The boy scowled at her for a moment, but then turned to leave, calling the other two to join him. After they were out of sight, Isa turned to Fig. "What is that thing?" she said, smiling, as she examined it.

"I want to help people with injuries get around better, so I took these two wheels and added a single chair between them. But to make it go, you have to push it. I am trying to find another way to sit in the chair and make it go from there."

"What do you mean, 'go from there'?"

Fig explained, "With only two wheels the chair has no stability, so I added a third wheel up front. I guess you could push the wheels on each side as you sat in it, but your hands will get dirty."

Isa put her hand to her chin as she said, "I see, you want the person sitting in it to make it go without someone pushing it."

"Yes, but not having help has slowed me down."

"If you can't use hands, what about using your feet?"

"Then, you would be going backward everywhere as you pushed. I will have to think about this problem for a while."

"Are you ok, really?" Isa asked in a softer tone.

"Yes, Isa, I am. Thank you for standing up to them, that was very brave."

"That IS what friends do."

"Yes, they do." Fig smiled. "Have you eaten? It is almost mid-day."

"I have not, but I am not here alone. My granny and friends are here also."

"Great, go bring them. We can get some food at the traveling wagon."

"You mean Eber?"

"You've already met him?"

"I met him earlier. He gave me a licorice root drink."

"He has food from the other kingdoms, very different and really good."

"I will go find them and meet you there."

Isa ran off to go and find her friends. Something in a shop caught her eye as she ran, and she stopped at the vendor. There, in the back of the shop was a cloak. Isa walked up and felt it with her hand. The material was soft yet seemed very strong.

A voice from behind said, "It was woven in the mountains of Moraii. The strongest material in all the land and extremely difficult to get. Do you like it?"

"I do. It's nice."

"Nice yes, but it's so much more." He took a dagger and tried to cut it. "Impenetrable material, they weave it extremely tight. It will protect you very well."

Isa looked closely at the Cloak. She really liked how it felt, but she had no way of buying it. "I'll speak with my granny and stop back by." She thanked him and continued on her way.

Kovack and Ynas walked around the vendors, Ynas looking for herbs and Kovack looking for anything unusual. They came across a gem vendor. He had many different gems, all rough cut, and needing to be polished.

Kovack said, "Ynas, look at these."

Ynas looked down at the gems. "Yes, but they do us little good until we find a blacksmith and gem mason to polish and set them."

"But a mine will be close by, that is good to know."

"Yes, we will have to gather the material. Isa will need light-weight armor studded with gems."

"I hope I have prepared her well enough for what lies ahead," Kovack said.

"I am not sure she will wear armor. She is as stubborn as you," Ynas said.

Kovack laughed. "But stubborn can be a good thing too, at times." Kovack looked down at Ynas and smiled. The old friends continued down the street. The next vendor had silk scarves and skirts made in vibrant colors.

"We get a scarf or skirt for Isa? "Kovack asked as he ran his hand over one hanging at the front of the store.

"I don't believe she would wear any of these." Ynas looked through all that the store had. "And they will not offer her any protection, but they are beautiful. Kovack, look at this." Ynas was pointing toward the next vendor. In his collection, he had many leather goods. Ynas was most interested in the belt hanging up-front. "Isa could use a belt like this. It has a pouch attached to carry her things close."

Kovack nodded as he looked over the belt. "Kovack agrees, Isa should have the belt."

"Very well." Ynas handed the vendor the money for the belt and then continued down the street.

Isa saw Kovack at the end of the street and ran over to him. She asked, "Find anything interesting?"

Kovack spun around, looked down at her, and with a curious look on his face said, "It seems like you have, lil one. What did you find?"

With a big smile, Isa answered, "I found a Cloak. It is finely woven and very soft. And I made a friend who invited us to join him for midday meal."

"A friend, already?" Granny chimed in. She stepped forward and reached her hands, holding the belt, wrapped it around Isa's waist.

Isa looked down, admiring the belt, "Oohh, that's nice! Thank you."

"A boy?" Kovack interrupted, looking even more curiously at Isa.

"Who is this boy, Isa?" Granny continued, "and how did you meet him?"

Isa explained, "I was exploring the shops. His shop is on the other side of town. On the way, I met Eber. He is a traveling um... vendor? I guess. That's where we will be eating. He brings food from many different places. Come on, let's go eat!"

Isa was excited and took Kovack and Ynas by the hand, leading them toward the center of town. "After we eat, we can check out the cloak. Then you can visit Fig's shop, he has the most incredible things there."

"Slow down lil one, Kovack does not walk as fast as you run. We will get there in time, Kovack is hungry."

"I could use a good meal myself," Ynas said.

They walked through the town till they came upon the wagon owned by Eber. Eber had set out tables and stools. Fig was sitting at the table nearest the wagon.

"Fig!" Isa called out to him and ran over to his table.

"Glad you made it, Isa," Fig said.

"Here is my friend Kovack and my granny, Ynas."

Fig bowed. "It is nice to meet you both."

"It is nice to meet you too," Kovack and Ynas both said as they both bowed.

Fig motioned toward the table. "Please join me at the table."

Kovack and Ynas took seats across the table from Fig, and Isa sat next to him. Isa began telling them about the adventure she had that day, just as Eber walked up.

"What will you be having today?" He saw Isa and smiled. "Back from your adventure so soon?" He winked.

"Not quite started yet, but I will," Isa answered. "Can we get some of your best food and drinks please?"

Eber said, "Of course, What kind are you looking for? I have food straight from Mount Moraii, hardest to get in all the land, and here just for you."

Ynas looked over at the excitement on Isa's face and said, "Yes, that sounds good, I'll have a small plate, please."

"I will have the same, but a slightly bigger plate if you don't mind," Kovack said.

"I'll have two plates for me, please," Isa said with a big grin.

Fig laughed. "A normal plate for me will do. And some of your special tea also for us all."

"Very well Fig, I'll be back shortly." Eber walked up into his wagon and began preparing the food." Isa continued telling the story of her day. After she was finished, Kovack and Ynas looked at each other and then back at her.

"It seems you had a busy day indeed, Isa. Fig, she said your father is a map maker but has been gone too long. Where did he travel to?" Ynas asked.

"He was traveling to Mount Moraii. It has little known about it. He wanted to add accurate maps into the records."

"Mount Moraii? Your father went up to that mountain?" Eber asked as he walked up to the table with their food. "That is not a good idea. They do not like visitors Fig."

Fig looked up at Eber and said, "My father is a kind man. They have nothing to fear from him."

"Some people don't care how kind you are," Eber said. "Not if you are trespassing. I hope they don't put him in their prison."

"What!" Fig exclaimed. "Why would they do that? Is that why he hasn't returned?"

"I am not sure. I have not heard rumors of such a thing, but I will look into it." Eber said as he set the plates down and returned a moment later with their drinks.

Ynas looked over at Eber and said, "You really should not speak of the bad things that may happen, until you can be sure of them. It is not fair to worry poor Fig."

"You are correct. I do not know," Eber said. "I will send my Nellie out with a note. I will find out if anyone may know where your father is. For now, eat your food and try to enjoy it."

The food was delicious, but Isa could see that Fig was restless and worried.

Kovack spoke up to break the silence, "So, Fig, Isa says you make many inventions? Kovack would like to see them." Fig was just twirling his fork in his food, sitting silently. "Fig? May Kovack see the things you make?"

Fig looked up. "Oh, sorry, yes, you may see them after we finish here if you would like."

"Thank you, Kovack would like that very much," Kovack said.

Fig smiled, but it was not a happy smile. When they had finished eating, Eber came back over to clear the table.

"How fast is your hawk, Eber?" Fig asked.

"She flies extremely fast. I should hear news of your father by tomorrow. I am sure he is ok, just busy making his maps," Eber said as he smiled turned and walked away.

Fig turned his head away from everyone and said, "I will not worry, I know my father, he is very smart, he is ok. We can go to my shop now if you are ready."

"First, we have a cloak to check out, then we go," Isa added. They walked back toward the shop where Isa had seen the cloak. "There it is!" shouted Isa.

"Do not get so excited, Isa," Kovack said, "we can't get a good price if they know you want it so bad."

"I'll check it out, Kovack," Ynas said as she walked up to the vendor. He was an old Goshan with a cane. Ynas smiled as she walked up to him. Isa tried to hear what her granny was saying but could not make it out. A moment later, Ynas walked back with the cloak.

"It is genuine and very high quality." She handed the cloak to Isa. Isa slid her arms into the cloak and wrapped it around her. "OOH, I really like it."

Ynas could not tell her no with that look on her face. She paid and thanked the vendor, then turned around and said, "Now we are off to Fig's shop. Lead the way."

Fig nodded and spun around, his thoughts still on his father. Fig walked slowly back toward his shop. Isa walked next to him talking the whole way. She had to try to cheer him up.

Kovack watched the two ahead of him. He was glad Isa made a friend. "Ynas, we should ask Fig to accompany us on our journey. We stop in Gosha, get the queen's help, then go to Moraii and speak with the King there. If Fig's father is a prisoner, we will work to get him freed."

Ynas nodded. "I agree, and a map maker would be a great help on our journey. So much has changed since I have been out that way."

They rounded the corner and walked into his shop.

"These are my ideas. I made them all," Fig said as he turned to face Kovack.

"You should see what he made outback!" Isa could not wait to show them. She took Kovack by the hand and pulled him.

"Kovack is coming, Kovack is coming, no need to pull."

Kovack's eyes grew wide. He had never seen such things. He tried to listen as Fig explained one after the other, but he really didn't understand most of it. Granny just smiled politely and nodded. She saw the imagination in Fig and could tell he would make wondrous things in his lifetime.

Kovack raised his hand, "These are amazing. Kovack never thinks of such things. You have quite an imagination. You should accompany us on our journey. We could use a map maker and um, an inventor. We will go to Gosha as planned, while there, the queen will help us get into Mount Moraii, where we will find your father. Eber's hawk will bring us news tomorrow. You can decide then if you will join us."

Isa exclaimed, "Yes, that's a great idea, Fig. We can help find your father and make sure he is safe."

Fig answered, "I don't know. I have never ventured too far away from the village before. But to find my father, I think I should." He sighed, "If the news comes back that he is in trouble, I will go. You may stay here tonight, bathe and get some rest. I don't have much, but you may share in what I have. For now, look around, see if you like anything."

"Kovack hasn't had a bath in um, never mind. I will go try," Kovack said.

Isa looked at him. "Yea, I can tell." Pinching her nose. They all laughed. "What about Kofang? We can't leave him out there alone."

"Who is Kofang?" Fig asked.

"He is a Draufganger from Darkwoods," Isa replied, "he has saved me more than once."

Fig thought for a moment, then walked over and opened a cabinet. He handed it to Isa and said, "Here, cover him in this blanket and walk him here, the villagers will think he is a pack animal."

"I don't like hiding him," Isa sighed. "But if it prevents a panic. I will go get him. Do you think he will take a bath too? I wonder how his fur would look without all those tangles."

"I will help you if you wish, or we can take him to Bur," Fig replied.

"Would Bur help him?" Isa asked.

"I believe he would, after all my father and I have done for him."

"That sounds great, I will go get Kofang and meet you back here." Isa hurried out the door with the blanket.

"I will go to Bur's and ask him to come here and help. You two can go upstairs and change. We can clean your clothes down here, and you can wear these until your clothes are ready."

Fig handed Kovack and Ynas some robes. "These are my father and mothers, I don't believe my father will mind, and my mother died years ago, so she won't mind. I will be back after I speak with Bur." Fig walked out the front door and down the street.

Kovack motioned to Ynas to go first.

Ynas giggled. "You are not scared of a little water, are you, Kovack?"

"Not water, Kovack does not fit well in small spaces. You go, Kovack will try after. Kovack will clean our clothes and set out to dry."

Ynas nodded and climbed the stairs. Kovack followed her up. They each chose a room and changed into the robes. Kovack took the clothes downstairs and washed them in a tub out back. When he was finished, he hung them on a rope to dry. Ynas took a while in the bath, it felt too good to rush. When she was content to come out, she put on the robe and walked into the room she had changed in earlier. The bed was soft, and it was not long before she was asleep.

Kovack walked into the bathing room. It was bigger than he expected. He fit into the tub rather easily. He thought to himself, oh now, how would he wash his hair? Might as well start, can't finish something ya don't start. He untied his hair and grabbed the soap.

7

Bathing the Beast

Fig walked in the front door carrying tools for Bur. "I can grab a chair from over here for you, and I have a big bucket out back."

"That will do, Fig, thank you. Now, where are my patients?" asked Bur.

"I'm sure they will be here soon," answered Fig.

Isa approached their camp and called out to Kofang, "Kofang, where are you! I wonder where he went, KOFANG…!!"

Kofang howled and began walking back from the woods. Isa heard him and waited at the camp until he returned. She checked the Hoofas and loaded the supplies back on them. "I might as well take everything back with me."

Kofang entered the camp.

"Were you out hunting?" Isa asked.

Kofang nodded.

"We are going into town. I would like you to wear this over you so we can join the others." Kofang looked at Isa a little confused, but he walked over to her. He had trusted her before; he may as well now.

Isa draped the blanket over him and placed a Hoofa on either side of him. "Walk between these three as I guide them into town."

Isa walked them down through the streets straight back to Fig's place. The streets were crowded, and no one seemed to notice them as they walked through the village. Isa tied the hoofas up in front of Fig's house and opened the door for Kofang to enter. Bur and Fig were standing inside.

"Here is your customer now," Fig said as they entered.

"Hello Isa, nice to see you again, but you didn't need any work done," said Bur.

"No, but my friend does," Isa said as she pulled off the blanket. Kofang raised his head and looked directly into Bur's eyes.

Bur stammered, "I, I...I have never worked on a...um, what is he?"

"He is not a what," Isa said. "He is Kofang of Darkwoods and he is my friend. Can you help with his fur? It is all matted. We are all getting cleaned up here before our long trip to Gosha."

Bur put his hand to his chin scratching it before saying, "I can try but is he ok with it? I don't want to hurt him but may not be able to avoid it."

Isa looked at Kofang. "Kofang, will you let Bur help you? I know you didn't trust the Tobu after they put you in the arena, but I trust Bur and Fig. I don't want people to see you as a beast anymore. Will you do this for me?"

Kofang whimpered. He had no desire for water, but she had saved him. He must try for her. Kofang let out a sigh and nodded.

"Oh, thank you!" Isa exclaimed as she hugged him.

Fig looked at Kofang. "He is much bigger than I expected. Um, well, I think we have a tub out back that is big enough, but I cannot carry it."

Bur walked around Kofang. "I will work on cutting and trimming his fur first, that will take me awhile. After I finish then we can work on cleaning him." Then he asked Kofang, "May I inspect your teeth?" Bur reached for Kofang's bottom jaw as he opened his mouth wide. "Wow, amazing teeth, and in excellent shape. Would you allow me to clean them?"

Kofang nodded.

Bur got out his tools and began cleaning each tooth carefully. "There you are, all bright and white. It seems you still have some baby teeth left. You are not very old, are you? I would say not even a season yet."

Isa couldn't believe it. "He is still growing!? Will he get bigger?"

"I don't believe he will get much bigger. He almost has a full set of adult teeth. You can tell by the size of the teeth. I don't have much experience with these, um, animals. But I have worked with the dogs we have around here, and I believe Kofang will grow in similar way."

Bur put his tools away and picked up his scissors. "Now for the hardest part, please remain as still as possible," Bur asked as he placed his hand on Kofang's shoulder.

He began trimming at Kofang's shoulder working his way down his back toward his tail. Little by little, the clumps of fur dropped off. Bur talked softly to Kofang as he worked, "You are shedding, that is helping this hair trim quite a bit." Kofang stood there wincing at each clip. Bur was concentrating hard, sweat pouring down his forehead. The pile of fur on the floor grew larger and larger as he worked his way down to Kofang's large paws.

"There, that should do it." Bur walked around Kofang inspecting his work. "I believe that is all," He said as he walked around one last time running his hands though the fur.

"Is the water ready?" Bur asked as he turned toward Fig.

Fig nodded. "Warm and ready."

Kofang turned to Isa. He had a frightened look on his face.

Isa walked up and put her hand on his forehead. She looked into his eyes and said, "It's ok, Kofang, it's just water. I will take a bath too after you are done." Isa walked with him out to the tub of water. "Alright, step inside." Kofang hesitated.

"Come on now, just a quick wash," Isa pleaded.

Kofang pulled back, knocking the things over behind him. He turned to run just as Kovack walked out the door.

Kovack grabbed him and set him in the tub, holding him tight. "Kovack washed, Kofang can too."

Isa yelled, "Start scrubbing quick!" Bur, Fig, and Isa all grabbed soap and rags. They scrubbed Kofang as Kovack held him. Kofang stamped and struggled, splashing them all.

"Time to rinse." Fig grabbed a bucket, filled it, and poured it over Kofang. The water splashed everyone.

"Hey!" They all exclaimed as they jumped back. Kofang shook, spraying them again.

"Hey!!" They all ran inside as Kofang shook again.

"Grab some rags to dry him!" Isa exclaimed.

"I don't think he will let us," Fig hollered back as they ran. Kovack tried grabbing Kofang, but he jumped around the backyard, occasionally shaking as he darted back and forth. Isa and Fig came running back with towels in their hands.

"Kofang!! Kofang!! Please hold still! Let me dry you now. You're all clean. It's all over, please come here! Kofang!! Please," Isa pleaded.

Kofang paused for a moment and turned his head toward Isa and whimpered.

"Please," she said softly. He walked over to her. He shook one last time, spraying a mist across her. She shook a little herself and started drying him with the towels. Fig was apprehensive at first but joined in drying Kofang. Isa rubbed and rubbed. She got up around his neck. His foot began to kick.

"You like that, huh?" She rubbed harder. He kicked harder. Isa laughed. "You're a funny one, Kofang. You like bathing, now, don't you?"

Kofang sighed.

"Well, at least the rubbing after." Isa finished up the drying and walked Kofang inside. "Now for a good final brushing." Isa grabbed a brush and got to work. After she finished, she stepped back. Kofang's fur was white with blue highlights. "Wow, you look amazing! I had no idea under that dark grey, dirty, matted fur you had such a beautiful coat of fur."

Isa stood there, amazed. Fig was speechless. Kovack stood there, staring.

Bur looked over at Fig and said, "My work is done."

"You did an amazing job, Bur," Fig said, "I had no idea."

Ynas walked down the stairs. "What's all the racket? Where's Kofang? And who is this!?"

"Granny, This IS Kofang,"

"Wow! Who would have known what a good hair trimming could do!" Ynas exclaimed.

Ono jumped down off Isa's shoulder and walked up to sniff Kofang. He sneezed. Kofang ignored him and walked over to a corner to lie down. All that made him very tired, and soon he was asleep. Ono walked over and curled up next to him.

"Time for my bath, I guess." Isa walked upstairs.

"I'm gonna need one too now," said Fig. He looked over at Bur. "I'll walk back to your shop with you. I need to talk about some things."

"Alright, let's go," Bur said, and he and Fig walked out the door.

Ynas motioned to Kovack, and they walked a little distance away from the house. She said, "We need to discuss our plans. Maybe Fig can design the weapons and armor we will need and even set the gems in them. When we get to Mt Moraii, we can acquire all the gems we will need."

"Yes, but can this boy design armor? And can you sense a gem in him?"

"I believe he can. He is not a warrior. More of an imaginative thinker. There is a stone that he can sync with. Not many know of it. I am sure we can find it in Mt Moraii."

Kovack asked, "What about the vendor here in town, did you notice the gem there?"

"I don't remember seeing it, but I wasn't looking for it really," Ynas answered. "We can go by and check for it on our way out of town tomorrow. For now, after all that excitement, I believe we get some rest and leave as soon as we hear from Eber tomorrow."

"Agreed." Kovack nodded. "Just look at this stuff. He has imagination. Kovack likes all this." Kovack found a seat on the far side of the yard. It had a nice view of the forest beyond. The wind was light with a sweet smell of the flowers that were just beginning to bloom. The clouds were rolling in slowly. He took a deep breath, and his eyes grew heavy. He loved the forest. It relaxed him, helped him forget the terrible things from before. The things he left behind.

Ynas walked inside and upstairs to check on Isa. Isa had just finished getting dressed after her bath.

Isa looked up as Ynas walked into the room and said, "Hello, granny, doesn't Kofang look amazing now?"

"Yes, it is as I have said before, try to look beyond what you see. People are not always as they first appear."

"Well, yes, I get it. But I always thought you meant who they are inside not the way they look after a haircut." Isa giggled.

"True, but don't underestimate how a haircut can make you feel so much better about who you are. I always taught you to take care of your body."

"I know. It is the only one I will get."

"Correct, but you will also feel much more confident when you take care of it. I believe we will see a big difference in Kofang now."

"I hope so. He is an amazing friend with a good heart. I wish he could see himself as I do."

"I believe with your help. He will. I will be getting some sleep now. You young ones wear me out. Do not stay up too late. Fig is a nice boy. You will have plenty of time to talk on our trip. And we will leave tomorrow."

"I will not be up long. I will wait for Fig to return and then get to sleep.

It was not long before Fig returned.

"That was quite an adventure," Isa said as he walked through the door."

He laughed a little. "Yea, I never would have imagined a day like today. It is good to have unexpected things happen once in a while."

"Are you ok, Fig. Really?"

"I am, Isa. Thank you for caring. We will find out about my father tomorrow, so I will not worry. I am exhausted, though. Kofang is stronger than I would believe possible. I have never seen such a Beast."

"He is not a Beast, he is my friend."

"He is a beast still, but I see kindness in him. He really likes you, Isa. You can get him to do anything."

"I am not sure about that, but everyone deserves a chance, or sometimes a second chance. I cannot believe how beautiful his fur is now. He looks amazing. and all because of a simple bath and haircut."

"That was no simple haircut. I am glad Bur agreed. My father and I do a lot of work for him, so he didn't mind returning the favor."

"I like Bur. He is a kind old Goshan. Have you been to Gosha?"

"I have only heard stories. We are far away from there, so I have not made the journey yet. I guess the time has come to go."

"Yes, we will know for sure tomorrow."

"I have already decided to go anyway. I feel I need to. We should get some sleep for now."

Isa nodded. They walked upstairs. Fig motioned goodnight and walked down the hall to his room. Kovack was asleep on the extra pad he gave him earlier. Fig quietly made his way to his bed. The thoughts of the day were still lingering in his head. His new friends were quite interesting. He smiled as his eyes closed, and he drifted to sleep.

<h1 style="text-align:center">8</h1>

<h1 style="text-align:center">Raiders in Andalusia</h1>

The morning sunrise shone through the window. The many little trinkets of glass hanging from the ceiling created colors of a rainbow reflecting all over the room. What a way to wake up every morning, Isa thought. She lay there admiring the colors until she heard noises downstairs. Someone was up already, probably Kovack. Isa sat up slowly. Granny was gone. That was normal. She stretched. It felt good not to sleep on the ground. Isa did not want to get up, but...today they started the next part of their adventure. And Fig was joining them. It was all too exciting. She jumped out of bed, and quickly got dressed, reached for her blades and paused. She really did not like the idea of fighting but sighed and strapped them on her side.

"Ono," she nudged him gently, "come on now." He curled up tighter. "Ok, no breakfast for you." She started out the door. Ono came running out and climbed up her taking his place on her shoulder. "I thought so." Isa laughed and walked downstairs. Everyone was gathered at the table.

Fig looked at Isa "I am glad you're up, I'll start breakfast." He began to prepare the meal.

Isa looked around. "Where's Kofang?"

"Out hunting," Kovack answered. "We start packing supplies while Fig cooks, getting an early start will help avoid unwanted attention."

"Alright, I'll get the hoofas ready." Isa walked out front.

The streets were still quiet. A few vendors were just beginning to open their shops. She walked around to the back and put the harnesses on the hoofas. She seemed to notice more than before. The Hoofas had large, kind eyes and were gentle. She was nervous before, but now she felt calmer and more relaxed with them. This was the first time she had harnessed them alone. She took her time, stroking the Hoofas long fur and talking to them as she worked. After the harnesses were on, she guided them around front and tied them to the hitching post. Kovack walked out with the packed supplies and set them on each Hoofa.

"We are one hoofa short now that Fig is joining us," Isa said.

"You ride Kofang. As you did yesterday. Ask him. He won't mind," Kovack answered.

Isa had preferred to ride Kofang anyway but did not want anyone to think she was nervous about riding a hoofa as she had been. They went inside and sat at the table just as Fig had finished cooking. Ynas had set the plates of food out for each person and after Ynas offered up a prayer for the food, they all began eating. Isa was not sure what was on her plate, but she tried it anyway. A bit hesitant at first, but it was good.

"Thank you, Fig, this is different."

"It is eggs I collect from our kip out back. And the bread and jam we get from shops down the street."

There was a knock on the door. Fig walked over and opened the door and let Eber inside.

"My Nellie has returned with a message. Your father was seen headed up to Mt Moraii many sunrises ago. He has not been seen coming back out, however we cannot confirm whether he is a prisoner. I have prepared some things here to help you on your journey. A package for each of you. For Ynas, many teas and herbs. For Kovack, some of my dried foods and some tools. For Fig, some difficult to find raw materials. And for Isa." He reached out his hands and placed a necklace on her. "This medallion will help you on your journey."

Isa held it in her hand. It was made of simple material, nothing fancy. She smiled and thanked him, but unsure how the medallion might help.

She looked back up at Eber. "What about Kofang?"

"Kofang? Who is Kofang?"

"He is a Draufganger from the Darkwoods," Kovack answered.

"A Draufganger, here? How did this happen?"

"He is my friend," Isa answered.

"I have never heard of a Draufganger being a friend to anyone. I am not sure of what I may give one."

Isa heard noise out back and rushed to the door to look. Kofang had returned.

"Kofang! Come in here, please." Kofang walked into the shop.

Eber's eyes grew wide. "He looks magnificent!"

"We asked Bur to come over and give him a trim and then we bathed him," Isa explained.

"You did an excellent job."

"Thank you," Isa said and then turned to Kofang. "Kofang, is it ok if I ride on your back now that Fig is joining us?" Kofang nodded.

Eber was astonished. "He understands you and responds? I'm impressed, Isa. I see that you do not have a harness, though. Will he wear one?"

Isa shrugged. "Ask him."

Eber turned to Kofang and asked, "Kofang, will you accept a harness from me so that Isa may ride on your back? I will bring it here to fit it. It is from another beast, but I believe it will fit with some adjustments."

Kofang looked a bit confused but nodded reluctantly.

"Great! I will be back shortly," Eber said and walked out the front door.

Kovack interrupted, "We need to get packed."

Fig walked over and started packing all his stuff in his bags.

After filling three bags, Kovack said, "Fig has no room for all that stuff, not on a Hoofa."

"Hmm, let me think," Fig said aloud. "If I use this strap, add these poles. I think I got it! My wheel invention! I can pull it behind the Hoofa. By adding the strap and poles to connect it to the harness. The Hoofa can pull more than they can carry."

"Yes, I think they can." Kovack nodded. "Ok, hurry up. Kovack will help."

It didn't take long till they were finished, and the new cart was loaded.

Eber returned with a small harness. It was made of leather and had a simple seat with long straps and stirrups on either side. He set it on Kofang and trimmed the straps, punched a few new holes, and fastened it in place.

"It is a lightweight harness used for the largest beasts of the north. With a little trimming, it fits well enough. You have hand-holds on the front of the seat and stirrups here. I will not put a bit in Kofang's mouth as a Hoofa would use. You will be able to keep stable as he runs and I believe, work well as a team now."

"Thank you, Eber, that is great!" Isa put a foot in the stirrup and swung her leg over Kofang's back. Eber adjusted the stirrups to Isa's legs and asked, "How does that feel, Kofang?"

Kofang gave a little shudder and took off at a slow run. Isa held on to the grips at the front of the small leather seat working on her balance. "Ok, I think I got it, Kofang, you can run a little faster now."

Kofang lunged forward.

"Not that fast! Not that fast!"

Kofang smoothed out his stride. Isa leveled out, sat up straight, then bent forward leaning close to Kofang. She could feel his breathing and his muscles flexing as he ran. She concentrated on moving in the saddle with his strides. "Ok, I think I'm getting it. But let's get back to the others."

Kofang turned and used a few trees to make a very fast turn leaving claw marks as his paws pressed against the tree trunk. Isa screamed, then giggled as Kofang darted even faster. Isa leaned in further, Kofang's fur was touching her nose now. A few more strides and they could see Fig's house. Kofang slowed his gait and walked around to the front to join the others. They were all packed and Fig and Kovack had finished the cart for all Figs supplies. Isa's hair was blown back, and she was wearing the biggest grin.

Fig turned as she approached. "Good, you're back. It looks like it went well, from that expression."

"Yes, I did not realize how fast Kofang can run, but I was able to hold on fairly well. This harness and saddle help a lot," Isa said with much excitement. "Thank you, Eber."

"We are ready now. Let's get started," Ynas said, "I will lead with Kovack up front."

They started slowly down the trail. As they put some distance from the village, they increased the speed, watching how Fig was doing in his cart.

"We are traveling slower than before, but I think we will be ok at this speed," Ynas said to Kovack. Who nodded and turned back to check on Isa.

Kofang bounded back and forth on the trail behind everyone. "She is getting good practice with Kofang," he said.

"She has improved her riding a lot already." Ynas smiled.

They rode in silence until the sun was high.

"We will stop here and eat," Kovack said, pulling his hoofa's reins. "Fig, get water for the Hoofas. Isa, let Kofang hunt while you set out food for everyone."

Isa dismounted, turned to Kofang and asked, "Will you be ok to hunt while wearing the harness?"

Kofang nodded and darted off. Isa pulled down the roll from one of the Hoofas and spread it out. She placed the bowls and food onto the mat. Fig finished watering the animals and set them to graze. They all sat and distributed the food amongst them.

"How do you like the ride so far, Fig," Isa asked.

"It is a bit bumpy, but I used a few rolls of bedding to sit on, which helps."

"Does your map show these routes we are taking?"

"Yes, we will be approaching the river by tomorrow, I think."

"River, what river?" Isa asked as she turned toward Kovack.

"It is the best way to cross the desert," Kovack explained, "It is a single river that winds through the desert. In the hottest times it dries up. We are in the growth cycle. The water is building so we will be able to get a ride on a ship there and head downstream."

"Yes, that is our plan, if the ships are traveling," Ynas added.

"Granny, you didn't say anything about a ship."

"I haven't told you of many things, lil one. It is easier to show you these things."

Isa was excited. A river, a ship, a desert, what else would she get to see?

"Finish up your food. We need to get moving," Kovack hollered.

They loaded up their supplies.

Isa called out, "Kofang! we are ready to go, are you ready?" He bounded out from the trees and walked over to Isa. Isa placed her foot into the stirrup and swung over into the saddle. "We are ready."

"Isa, go ahead of us and scout the trail," Kovack said, "be careful, and don't go too far."

She nodded and bounded off on Kofang.

"She needs the practice and was really wanting to run, so, we can let her," Kovack said to Ynas, who shook her head and climbed up onto her Hoofa. They started slow, letting Fig get his stride. The road narrowed and they were forced into a single row. The trees were getting thicker around them. It was difficult to see far in front of them now as the trees closed over the trail and the sun was blocked out.

Isa came back down the trail. "The road is blocked ahead. Looks like a tree fell. It must have been there for some time now, the vines have grown over it."

They continued down the trail until they came upon the tree and dismounted.

Kovack walked over to the tree, looked around and said, "This tree did not fall. It was placed here. These vines grow fast, maybe this tree has been here for two sunrises. Someone is trying to block the trail."

"Why," Isa asked.

"Not sure," Kovack answered. He reached down and with a big heave, picked up one end of the tree and thrust it off the trail. The trees rustled and a net fell on Kovack. Another net was flung over Isa and Kofang. The yells filled the air as the figures all jumped out of the trees grabbing Fig and Ynas. Many of them held Kovack down, while others jumped on Kofang.

Isa was trapped under the net with Kofang. She reached down and grabbed her blades and cut through the net, jumped clear, took her stance, and yelled, "Let my friends go!" Her weapons began to glow deep red, the glow moved up her arms and enveloped her body. She charged toward the group holding her granny, knocking them back.

"Who are you and why are you doing this!" The red glow grew even brighter.

She darted across to Kofang cutting the net open big enough for him to free himself, then she freed Fig. Red flashed with each hit. She knocked the two men holding Fig back into the trees then turned toward Kovack, who had stood up despite the three men trying to pin him down. Isa screamed and charged, the net split, Kovack ripped it open and threw one of the men across the trail. The remaining men scattered and ran back into the trees disappearing from sight. Isa was breathing hard, her chest heaving. She screamed again. Kofang howled and as he started to leap into the trees to chase them, Isa flung herself onto the saddle and disappeared into the trees.

"Isa, stop! Let them go!" Kovack yelled after her, but Isa was gone.

He looked at Ynas. "Do you think they have reopened The Arena?"

Ynas sighed, "I hope not. We need to be more careful though. After Moraii, maybe we should go check on the Arena."

"Agreed," Kovack said, then turned to Fig, "Fig, are you ok?"

"I am, but what was that with Isa? How did she glow red?"

"We can explain later, for now we need to get out of here, as soon as Isa returns," Kovack answered.

"We have time now," Fig insisted, "how did Isa glow?"

"Isa has synced with the ruby, the gem of courage and emotion," Ynas explained, "I have the emerald which enables me to heal. We can explain in detail later how to sync, but it starts inside you. Your personality, your heart, your mind. The gem you sync with depends on what is most important to you. It will enhance your natural abilities considerably."

"Can I sync with a gem?"

"Not everyone can, but I believe you will be able to," Ynas explained, "we can explore this when we are in Gosha. They will have the information you will want. You have a great imagination. I believe you will sync with the topaz. Many gems can be found in Mt Moraii. We can get topaz there if we can't find one earlier. You will have much studying to do first though."

"I will study as hard as needed," Fig exclaimed, "That was so awesome!"

Isa and Kofang came back leaping through the forest. "The forest got too thick to follow them any further. Why would they attack us? Kovack?"

"Maybe they started the arena again. They grab people and beasts to sell to the arena for battles. If you want to be free, you must win."

"Arena?" Isa looked puzzled. "Where is this arena?"

"At the edge of the desert, down the river, then off to the right a half day ride," Kovack answered.

"How do you know of this arena?"

"I fought there." Kovack walked over and mounted his Hoofa. "No more questions, we need to go!"

Everyone mounted up and slowly started back down the trail. Isa ran out front, scouting ahead. She saw no signs of the raiders. They increased the pace and soon came out of the woods into a clearing where they moved up riding beside each other.

Kovack yelled out, "Stay alert! We need to keep riding until we reach the river, pick up the pace, We are not safe yet."

"You said we would reach it tomorrow!" Isa yelled back.

"We would have, but after that attack, we need to make it tonight. Hurry up!"

Kovack kicked the Hoofas hindquarters and the Hoofa took off, Ynas did the same. Isa and Kofang darted forward. Fig snapped the reins. His Hoofa lunged forward as he bounced around in the chariot he had built, he snapped the reins again and the Hoofa ran even faster. They raced down the trail till the sun was setting and off in the distance, they could see the river.

The forest opened to a sandy shoreline and Kovack pulled the reins to slow the Hoofas. In the slow-moving waters were reflections of orange, yellow, and red from the setting sun. Floating at the end of a dock was beautifully carved ship with a beast head at the front as if it were guiding it. Many large oars hung out of holes on each side. The tail of the boat rose as high as the head and rolled into a ball at the tip. They slowed to a stop and dismounted the Hoofas near the river's edge.

9

A Ride Down the River

Kovack walked down the dock and aboard the ship. No one was in sight. "Anybody here?" he called out, but there was no answer.

He walked to the door leading to the lower deck and knocked. He waited for a moment and when no one answered, he opened the door. The dimly lit room had only a few crates to the left and candles mounted in the four corners. Jeering, yelling, and laughter were coming from behind a door at the opposite side of the room. He walked over and knocked loudly.

The noise stopped and a deep voice called out, "Enter!"

Kovack walked inside. Four men were sitting around a table, and more men were sitting behind them on stools against the walls. They all remained silent as Kovack entered.

"What are ya needing there, sir?" the big Goshan man at the end of the table stood up as he asked.

Kovack scanned the room and then answered, "We need a ride across the desert."

"We?"

"Yes, five of us, three Hoofas and a cart."

The man leaned forward putting both his hands on the table. "Really? And do you have ya some coins? We here need to eat."

Kovack pulled out a leather pouch and tossed it on the table. "We do. Can you take us? No questions asked."

The Goshan man raised his eyebrow, glanced at the pouch on the table and said, "Take a seat, let's see what you got."

Kovack looked down at the game in progress on the table. "Kovack has not played for a long time, forgot how."

"Yea, well, I forgot how to maneuver this ship," the man responded as he sat down.

Kovack sat down reluctantly and began to study the stones laid out across the table. They were polished and of different size and colors with symbols carved on each side of the stone. He tried hard to remember the rules.

A crew member slid his stones in front of Kovack and reset the stack in the center of the table. He explained, "Ya stack the stones according to the color or carving. Pass if you can't play a stone and do not let the pile fall or ya lose. And ya cannot pass if you can match a stone, so no cheatin. Ya win when you're the first to play your last stone. Now don't ya go losing my hand now that I given it to ya."

Kovack nodded as he examined the stones in front of him. He had never tried playing this game on a boat before. The boat swayed as he placed a stone on the stack. Each player took their turn stacking a stone. Kovack's hand was shaking as he reached across the table with another stone. He set it on the top slowly, still holding it. He steadied himself and let go of the stone. The pile swayed back and forth but settled without falling.

"Well done, sir." The big man eyed Kovack intensely.

The players each took turns setting a stone until Kovack had one stone remaining. The big man had two. They glared across the table at each other. The next player set his stone. Kovack may have only been down to his last stone but setting the previous stone had been difficult enough.

The big man set his stone. "Only one left," he snickered. The pile swayed and stopped.

The next crew member set his stone. It was Kovack's turn. The sweat was dripping down his forehead. He took a breath and thought, This is it, if I can set this last stone, I will win.

The boat rocked making the stones sway. He waited for the boat to settle, extended his hand, and held the stone over the pile. Kovack lowered his hand slowly holding his breath. When the stone touched the top of the pile, he set it down and removed his fingers. The pile swayed for a moment and then steadied.

"Kovack is out of stones. Looks like Kovack wins."

The big man glared at him and laughed. "Yes, you did. Well done. . .well done." All the crew cheered.

"This game is not half as fun when played on dry land. I am Captain Maku. We have an empty cargo room you and your friends can take. We can leave tomorrow at first light, so long as the river continues to swell at the rate it is."

"Thank you. I will bring in my friends," Kovack said, "and remember, no questions."

"Very well," replied Captain Maku.

Kovack walked off the ship and out to the group and raised a finger. "I do not trust this captain yet. He will take us, and he has the only ship, and this is the only way down the river. All of you need to remember to keep quiet. Do not speak of where we go or why. Do you understand?" They all nodded. Then he looked at Fig. "Especially you, about your father."

He walked over to Kofang. "My friend, I ask that you be patient, it will be hardest for you."

Kofang growled a bit. They walked the Hoofas one at a time aboard the ship. There was a ramp in the back leading down to the lower level. Kovack opened the door to the room they would stay in. It was mostly empty with only a few supply crates lining one wall, but no beds or chairs.

After they all entered the room and closed the door, Kovack said in a low voice, "I will check with the captain about food. We need to get the Hoofas tied and settled. "Kofang, can you go hunt and get some meat for a few days' journey? Be careful."

Kofang nodded and quickly left the ship.

Fig and Isa pulled out their supplies. "Looks like we will be ok for the trip, but not for long after," Isa said.

Kovack sighed, "Kovack does not like being low on supplies. I hope the captain is generous. I will be back shortly. Isa, come with me, please." Kovack walked back to the room where all the crew members were.

Captain Maku was about to set his last stone to win the game as Kovack entered the room. Kovack stopped and waited for Maku to finish his move.

"Ha, I win again!" Captain Maku exclaimed, and the crew cheered. He looked up and asked, "And who is this?

Kovack grunted, "No questions, remember?"

"I do, but, such a beautiful young lady on a big rough ship, I gotta ask. And that hair. I haven't seen hair like that since… well, I don't remember. No matter. Hello young lady, do I have permission to know your name?"

"I am Isa. Nice to meet you, captain. Your ship is magnificent."

"Thank you, you have excellent taste. What may I do for you?

"Do you have food and drink on such a fine vessel for your guests?"

"Guests? Of course." Captain Maku motioned to a crew member. "See to it that our guests get some food and drink, only the best will do for them."

Isa bowed her head slightly and turned, following the crew member out. He was a tall, lanky boy, not much older than she was.

"I am Azdaja."

"Nice to meet you, Azdaja," Isa said, "where are you from?"

"I came from the forests far in the south."

"How did you end up here?"

"I wanted to travel and see the land, what better way than by ship. After I save enough coin, I will head north to see what lies beyond the desert."

Isa wanted to talk about the maps Fig had of that area but remembered Kovack's words and instead said, "That sounds like a nice plan."

"Where are you from?" Azdaja asked.

"Oakheart?" Isa paused. It couldn't hurt to talk a little, she thought.

"Oakheart? That's Tobu territory. Why would a Naslov be in Tobu Territory?"

"What do you mean? My Granny raised me there and it's a nice area."

"True, but we come from much farther in the forest."

"We?" Isa asked.

"Yes, the Naslov kingdom is much farther west from there," Azdaja explained. "It's where I came from. You are Naslov, your family had to come from there, too."

"I don't know anything about the Naslov." Isa looked confused. She took the food he was holding and turned in a hurry to leave. "I've got to go." She walked quickly back the room and closed the door hard behind her.

Ynas could see in Isa's face something was wrong. "Are you ok?"

Isa looked at her Granny. "Who are the Naslov?"

"We are. Where did you hear that name?"

"From Azdaja, the young boy who gave me this food. He said he is from the kingdom deep in the forest."

"That is where we are from as well. During the war, I was of great service to the Tobu kingdom. I could not return to the Naslov kingdom after your mother fell in battle. At my request, King Beylor allowed me to settle in Oakheart at the edge of his territory. Many of our people joined me there. We found a peaceful place away from all the aftermath of the war while they rebuilt the four kingdoms."

"So, I am Naslov? What does that mean?"

"The Naslov are one with Nature," Ynas began explaining. "They are natural fighters and seem to flow like water as they move so effortlessly in any fighting form. They are the tribe who first learned Tree speak and can bend nature to their will using the amethyst. I have taught you much of this. You know who you are. The remainder you may now begin to learn. Kovack can teach you much of the Naslov. His best friend, your father, was one."

"I can't believe what I am hearing!" exclaimed Isa, "Not many moons ago there was only our village, small and quaint. There were no four kingdoms, races, or even tree speak. How much more don't I know?!"

Ynas answered, "A lot. But you didn't need to before. The land of Andalusia is much bigger than any of us know."

"I am so confused my head hurts. It's all too much! I am going to sleep. If I can." Isa walked over to a corner and rolled out her mat and pulled Ono down off her shoulder.

"Sing me a song my little friend." Ono began to purr in a rhythm. Isa hummed along with him. Kofang walked over and laid beside Isa. The warmth of his fur comforted her, and she slowly fell asleep.

The ship heaved as the wave hit waking everyone. Isa got to her feet, picked up Ono and yelled, "What's happening!?"

"The river swells with the new rain, time to go!" a crewmember yelled back.

Kofang was up already. "Stay here!" Isa said to Kofang as she ran out the door and topside of the ship. She could see the swells of water coming from upstream, one after the other. The river increasing in depth with each swell.

"Man the oars!! Every man to their station quickly!!" Captain Maku yelled.

The crew members were running across the ship and to their places. Isa was just trying to stay out of the way. She focused on the river as it moved with each swell. She felt her body move with the water. A feeling of calm swept over her. Far off in the distance she could see dark clouds that were the source of the swells. She stood there for some time as the crew scrambled to get the ship turned and headed down the river.

The crew pulled hard on the oars as the first mate called out orders. The ship had straightened, and the crew used the oars to steady the ship. Captain Maku had the wheel firm in his grip.

"The first swells of the season are the most exciting!" he yelled to Kovack.

Kovack nodded as he stood beside him watching everything around him intently. The desert sand seemed endless on either side. Some dunes were several times as tall as the height of the river.

Captain Maku explained, "In full season, when the river is at its highest, we can look straight across the desert. You chose a great time to head down river, can be dangerous though, if those dark clouds catch us."

Kovack turned to look behind them. He could see flashes of lightning in the clouds off in the distance "Will we stay in front of them?" he asked.

"Most likely, I have been caught only once before," Maku answered. "If a strong wind picks up, the rain will catch us. Then, the real fun begins. For now, hold on to the rail."

Kofang had never been on a ship before, his stomach turned with every heave.

"Kofang, are you ok? You don't look so good," Ynas asked as she walked over to check on him. She placed her hands on each side of his head. Her hands glowed green as she closed her eyes and concentrated. She withdrew her hands after a few moments. "You should feel better for the remainder of the trip now. But take it easy."

Kofang nodded and walked over to a corner to lie down. There was too much going on above. He wanted no part of this crew.

The ship continued to lurch with each swell, though the swells were smaller now. Kovack walked over to Isa and suggested, "You should practice fighting on moving ground. Feel the sway of the ship as the water swells. Your skills will improve a lot."

"I do already. I feel the water as it rushes past us. I smell the moisture rising in the air as the storm closes in on us. The storm will catch us before we reach our destination."

"You sure?"

"Yes, it is moving much faster than us. I feel the wind coming."

"You feel all this already? Well done. I will go tell the captain. Maybe he can make the ship go faster. You try to concentrate on your training."

Isa closed her eyes and concentrated harder. She began moving through her fighting stances as the ship lurched. Though not easy at first, it did not take her long to feel one with the ship. She jumped up onto the rail and found her balance as the ship swayed. Isa closed her eyes and began going through her fighting stances.

"What are you doing!?" Azdaja yelled as he ran over to Isa.

Isa stumbled, turned, and began falling backwards over the rail waving her arms frantically.

Azdaja grabbed her cloak and pulled her back in. "What were you thinking?!" he yelled at her.

"What were YOU thinking!?" she yelled back. "Never interrupt my training, I should knock you out right here!"

"You were going to fall,"

"I was not!" said Isa sternly. "I can feel the ships movements and move with it. Just watch. And keep silent!" She was still upset. Isa closed her eyes, took a few deep breaths, calmed herself and began to feel the ships movements again. She concentrated deeper and when she was ready, she opened her eyes and jumped up on the rail.

Azdaja called out, "Careful…!"

"Sshhh!" Isa walked down the rail, turned, and walked back. She took her stance and began her training once more while Azdaja looked on in amazement.

A Naslov this young should not be this advanced yet, he thought. He could feel the waves and the storm moving in, but he never tried such a daring thing. I better work harder on my training, he thought. He had stopped training since boarding the ship last season, he didn't want anyone on the ship to discover his abilities.

"AZDAJA!! Back to your post!" Captain Maku yelled.

Azdaja snapped out of his thoughts and ran back to his post.

Kovack walked up to the captain and said, "This storm is moving faster than us and will catch us."

"And how do you know this?" asked Maku.

"Isa has felt it, she is Naslov," Kovack explained.

"Naslov, you say…?" He sighed. "I have sailed this river for over twenty seasons and can read the weather better than any Naslov, especially a female who is not yet mature."

"Do not be mistaken," interrupted Kovack, "she is more mature than you think. It would be wise to heed her."

Captain Maku scratched his head. "I will consider speeding up the ship, however, I cannot risk tiring out my crew."

"Kovack will row. Kofang, Fig and Isa can help, too," offered Kovack.

"Very well." Captain Maku turned and commanded, "MAN THE OARS, FULL SPEED AHEAD!"

The crew hurried to the seats at the oars, picked up the oars and looked to the first mate and yelled, "Ready!"

The First mate yelled, "Ready all...Row! PULL...PULL... PULL!" The ship picked up speed with every stroke. They rowed for hours until they began to collapse from fatigue.

Kovack went down into the room and said, "Kofang, Fig, I need you to row with me. Ynas, can you look after the men? They are exhausted. We need to keep the speed up to stay ahead of the storm."

They went below deck and took up the oars. Isa walked in and grabbed one next to Kofang. "We pull together" She looked at him and smiled.

"Pull...pull...pull!" Kovack called out the commands. "Give way together. Pull!"

"What does that even mean?" asked Fig.

"You all need to pull the oars in unison," Kovack replied, "it's ship talk."

"Where did you learn ship talk?" asked Isa.

"Watching the first mate on the ship."

Isa shook her head and they continued rowing.

They pulled hard for hours until the captain came down and said, "My crew will take over shortly. Get some rest. Food is being served on deck so you can enjoy the view." They let go of the oars.

"I feel like I'm still rowing," Fig said as they walked up to the deck.

"Me too," added Isa.

"Good, then row the food into your mouth." Kovack laughed.

"Ha...ha," Isa said sarcastically.

The food was set up on tables at the ship's bow. The sun was setting, and the desert seemed to catch on fire.

"The storm may still catch us, but we are moving as fast as the current will allow us. Let us enjoy a meal for tonight, rest up and face tomorrow when it comes," said Captain Maku as waved to one of his crew.

The young lad pulled out a flute and began playing some music. Isa remembered these sounds from her village. The flute had always calmed her. With the storm behind them, the air smelled fresh, and the sunset was magical. Isa decided to enjoy the moment she had right now. The food was so delicious that she ended up eating a bit too much and let out a burp.

"Excuse me," she said.

"Nice one," exclaimed Captain Maku, as he let one out of his own. The crew began to burp all over the ship followed by laughter.

"My crew is fearless, but without much manners, I suppose."

The captain brought out his fiddle and began to play and the dancing began. The footsteps were like thunder on the deck as they stamped their feet in rhythm. Song after song he played. Isa enjoyed watching the dancing that lasted until the first moonrise.

"We all best be getting some sleep. Azdaja, take the wheel. You four, man the oars. Keep her steady and just faster than the current. We will take over in the morning," Captain Maku ordered. Azdaja took his place at the wheel. Everyone else went down to their rooms to get some sleep. Isa was so exhausted, but happy. She curled up with Ono and closed her eyes. For two days they rowed taking turns as they did the first day, the storm closing in on them with each passing day. On the third day, it began to rain. The storm had caught them.

Captain Maku said, "We will be at our destination by tomorrow. We just need to stay in front of it one more day."

"That's not gonna happen," Kovack answered. "We need to prepare for the worst."

Captain Maku yelled, "Tie everything down! Prepare the lashes. Everyone on board must be prepared to tie down in a hurry. Wear these ropes around your waist. Hook into the lashes when things get rough."

The rain grew heavier, lightning lit up the sky. The dark clouds were overtaking them, turning the day into night. The howling of the wind became deafening.

"Every man to the oars!! Row as if your life depended on it!!" Captain Maku hollered.

"Captain! captain! I have an idea," Fig yelled, "I have this cloth here. I can use it to harness the wind. We will move much faster!!"

"What have we got to lose! Do it!" Captain Maku yelled back before turning to Kovack. "Kovack, help him!"

Fig and Kovack worked as fast as they could.

"Why not think of this sooner? Would have helped," Kovack asked.

"Yes, but not all ideas are instant," Fig explained. "Lash this here, attach the rope there. Make sure it is tied tight."

"Kovack knows how to tie."

The two tied quickly and fastened the rope to the head of the ship.

"That should do it, Kovack. Release it slowly!!" Fig said

Kovack wrapped the rope around the hand and released the chute. The wind filled it and yanked it forward. The rope burnt Kovack's hand as the chute took off. Kovack gripped tighter and tried slowing the rope. Just a little more and the rope would be taught.

"Good job!!" Fig said as the ship lurched forward with the new wind power. Fig was thrown back under the momentum. Kovack still had his hands on the rope and reached over to grab Fig.

"We need to tie off, Fig!" he said as he pulled him toward the lashes.

"You need to get your hands healed!" Fig hollered back.

The captain struggled to hold the wheel straight. He laughed aloud. "I have the fastest ship ever!" He looked over at the crew. "Put up the oars!! You men get tied off! Everyone get down below or tie off immediately. As fast as the ship was cutting through the water, the storm still closed in. The rain beat down on the deck.

Kovack made his way down the stairs to get to Ynas, his hands were badly burnt from the rope. Fig held onto his cloak and followed him downstairs. The wind howled louder. The lightning flashed across the sky right above them and the thunder was deafening.

Captain Maku was yelling and cheering, "YEA, THIS IS THE WAY!! IS THAT ALL YOU GOT!! He let out a loud yell. The swells of water came rushing behind them. The boat surged forward faster with each gust of wind.

"This is crazy!" Azdaja was tied to the rail at the stern, looking back at the storm that was overtaking them. The rain hit him hard as the wind swept it across the ship. "We are not going to make it!!" he yelled. But no one heard him over the thunder.

Below deck, Ynas worked at healing Kovack's hands. The Hoofas were terrified and stamped their feet and pulled at their ropes. Isa tried to comfort Ono but was nervous herself. Kofang was beginning to feel sick again. The ship was tossing back and forth as it surged forward.

After Kovack's hands were healed, he headed up to help Captain Maku at the wheel. As he walked up the stairs, he could see the river turned ahead. He turned and yelled to the captain, but Maku could not hear him. He pointed ahead. The captain looked over the bow and seeing the bend in the river ahead, he tried to turn, but the wind chute was pulling the boat too hard.

"Cut the rope!!" Captain Maku yelled. But Kovack could not hear him. "Cut the ROPE!!" he yelled louder as he motioned an ax chop with his arm. Kovack turned and pulled out his axe. He rushed forward and with a quick swing, set the chute free.

The ship began to slow immediately, but not soon enough. Captain Maku turned the wheel with all his strength. The ship began to turn, but as they headed into the corner, the waves hit and threw the ship forward over the embankment Ynd across the sand. It slid for what seemed forever before coming to a rest. The crew below deck had been thrown forward when it hit. Everyone tied to the lashes were flung violently back and forth until it came to a rest. Kovack had been thrown over the front of the ship upon impact and rolled out of the way just in time as the ship slid past him. Captain Maku slammed into the wheel and was hurt, but not terribly bad. Isa and Ynas slammed into the hoofas as they were thrown into the wall. The storm raged on, pounding the ship for hours as it passed by them.

"I will need to begin healing immediately. It is only fair that I first heal the beasts that saved us." She began with the hoofas. Then Kofang who was shaken, but ok. When she finished, she made her way room to room healing as she went.

"Isa, go find Fig and Kovack? I can finish up here."

Isa nodded and ran up the stairs. The wind was so intense, she thought it would blow her away. She could see Captain Maku lying across the wheel and the other crew members laying on the deck, still tied. She did not see Kovack anywhere.

"Kovack!!"..."Kovack!!" she yelled.

"He was thrown over the front when we hit." The voice came from near her feet. She could barely hear it.

Isa knelt down. "What, Fig! Oh, Fig, are you ok?"

"Yes, but let's not do that again. . .ever!" He groaned.

"Agreed," Isa said as she helped him to his feet, "let me help you down to my Granny, she'll heal you."

Fig held his side as Isa helped him to his feet. "I can make it. You go find Kovack, he is still out in this storm."

"Are you sure?" Isa saw concern in Fig's eyes. "OK," she said reluctantly and walked to the edge of the ship.

The wind was even stronger on the sides. The ship was half buried in the sand. She could jump down with ease, but as strong as the wind gusts were, she decided to make her way to the stern. She couldn't see far with the rain blowing into her. As she jumped down into the rain-soaked sand, her feet sunk down past her ankles. Each step was a chore, but she made her way back toward where the ship left the river. She pulled the cloak over her head tight and closed her eyes to concentrate. Kovack, where are you? She hoped he would hear her thoughts. She blocked out the storm. Kovack...Kovack, please answer, but she couldn't feel his presence. She stumbled forward hoping to feel his presence as she went. Near the riverbank, as her foot sunk into the ground, she felt a flash shoot through her.

"Kovack!" she yelled and fell to her knees and began digging until she felt a cold hand. "NO, Kovack!!" she screamed, "Get up!"

She dug frantically. Where was his head? She dug his arm out following it to his shoulder. He was pale and cold. The rain began to collapse the sand around the hole as she dug. "NOOO!!" Isa screamed as she dug as fast as she could, tears streaming down her face. But the water was filling the hole almost as fast as she could dig. A red aura began surrounding Isa, glowing brighter as she dug.

"KOVACK!!" She smacked him across his face. Time seemed to stand still. The red aura expanded as a bubble, disintegrating the raindrops around them. "WAKE UP!!"

Kovack coughed. "Why did Isa hit Kovack?" He coughed again.

"Get up! Hurry! The water is rising!" Kovack heaved a deep breath and pushed up with his arms. His body raised slowly out of the wet sand. He rolled out of the hole he had been in and lay on his back for a moment.

"Ow…" he groaned.

"Ow? Is that all?" Isa exclaimed

"That hurt, so yes, ow," Kovack answered.

Isa shook her head. "You're unbelievable."

"Thank you for coming for me," Kovack said in a low voice.

"Ow?" Isa laughed and shook her head again. "You're welcome. Can you make it back to the ship?"

"Don't think so, not yet."

"We shouldn't stay here."

"You go, Kovack will get there. The rain will stop. It's ok."

"Yea…no, not gonna happen," Isa said as she used her cloak to cover them both. She was too exhausted to make it back herself. Kofang would come for them. She knew he would. She fell asleep across Kovack's chest.

She woke to a nudge. Kofang had come. The sun was out now that the storm had passed. Isa tried to move and found that everything hurt.

"Ow," she said and quickly turned to Kovack after thinking of what she had just said.

"Yes, Ow," he said and then laughed. Ow...ow...ow. Don't make me laugh. Big ow."

Isa laughed along with him as she slowly climbed onto Kofang. She looked back toward Kovack and said, "I'll send my granny after I get to the ship. Come on, Kofang, let's hurry." Kofang leapt forward towards the ship.

Kovack looked up at the sky. In all his years, he had never crashed so magnificently. He smiled as he laid in the wet sand next to the big hole he had rolled out from the night before. After every storm, there is beautiful peace, he thought to himself as he took a deep breath and closed his eyes to rest.

Kofang leapt up on the boat. Isa jumped off and ran over to her granny, who was healing Captain Maku as he lay slumped over the wheel.

She yelled, "Granny, granny! Come quickly, I found Kovack, and he's hurt really bad!"

"I will go as soon as I am done here," Ynas said without looking up. "All these men are hurt badly from the crash. I'll get to Kovack as soon as I can."

"But it's Kovack! He almost died!" Isa exclaimed.

"Is he awake?"

"Yes, but..."

"Did he say anything?"

"He said, Ow."

Ynas laughed. "He will be fine, lil one. I will be there soon. Please check the men on deck here for serious injuries, they will need healing first."

After Ynas finished healing the most seriously wounded crew members, she called to Kofang, "Kofang, will you carry me to Kovack, please?" Kofang nodded and she climbed up into the saddle. "Easy now, I am not as agile as Isa."

Kofang leapt down into the sand as softly as he could and carried Ynas over to where Kovack lay.

Ynas dismounted and knelt down next to Kovack. "How are you my old friend?"

Kovack opened his blue eyes and turned his head toward Ynas. "I am ok, nothing a bit of rest won't fix."

"I believe it is a bit more serious than rest alone would handle." She placed her hands over him and they started to glow green. Ynas worked on Kovack for some time before Isa came walking with Fig.

"Will he be ok?" Fig asked.

Ynas answered, "Of course, after a few days' rest, he will be just fine." Ynas stood up and turned around. "Help him to his feet. We need to get him to a dry place."

"We can't lift him back onto the ship," Isa remarked. Kofang walked over to Kovack and pushed his head into Kovack's shoulder. Kovack rolled over and pushed up onto his knees. Then, using Kofang to help himself, he placed a foot forward and pulled himself to a standing position. Kovack placed a hand on Kofang's back and walked beside him as they made their way back to the ship. The ship had been buried deep in the sand but was still too high to climb up, so Isa called to the captain, "Captain Maku! Can you help us aboard!"

Captain Maku looked over the side then yelled, "Hold on a sec!"

Isa could hear the men moving around for a while until, over the side dropped a plank and some crates. A few crew members jumped over and got to work building a ramp up to the Deck.

"Won't take too long ma'am," a crew member yelled down to Isa.

"Thank you," she yelled back.

When the men finished, they all boarded the boat. Kofang walked Kovack back to their room. Kovack laid down and was asleep before long.

"We will all need some rest after all that excitement. The river will take a while to rise high enough to get this ship back into it. We will need the time to inspect it and make any repairs needed," Captain Maku said.

Ynas said, "We will rest here until Kovack is better and then we will continue on with the Hoofas. I think I have had enough of river rides for a while. I am exhausted after healing everyone, I will need to rest awhile myself. Isa, you, and Fig may help the crew if you like, I will see you in the morning." Ynas walked down into their room to rest.

Fig looked at Isa and asked, "Should we help inspect the ship?"

"We can, but does anyone know where we are?" Isa asked

Captain Maku answered, "We are not far from the dock we were aimin to reach. The desert ends half a day's ride further downstream. Other boats will begin passing us before long."

"Are we safe here?" Isa asked as she looked over the rail.

"As safe as anywhere, as long as I'm around." Captain Maku winked.

Isa looked at him and shook her head.

He explained, "Isa, it is too early for most ships to sail, the um... traders will not get back upriver till the current slows, unless they cross the desert, and that is rare. The river becomes more dangerous after it fills, and the current slows. Until then, you're safe."

"I have more questions now. These 'um... traders,' who are they and how is a calm river more dangerous than what we just faced?" Isa asked

"Too much to explain, just know you are safe, that's all." The captain turned to leave.

Isa was confused, but she turned and motioned to Fig, and they jumped down off the side of the ship. Azdaja was inspecting the front of the Ship.

Isa asked, "What are you looking for?"

Azdaja explained, "The impact may have weakened the main center beam. I do not see any signs of damage though. We wouldn't want to sink after getting back into the river, would we?"

"Guess not," Isa said as she placed her hand on the ship and walked down the side inspecting as she went. Fig followed doing the same.

After they walked around the whole ship, Fig said, "The moon is rising, I am sure we checked the whole ship. I am tired. I think we should get some rest."

"I agree, come on Ono, let's get back aboard huh?" They made their way back to the room and quietly slid into their beds.

The next morning, as the crew slept late, Azdaja packed a bag and slipped off the ship and began walking downstream. By the time anyone noticed he was gone, the wind had blown away any sign of him.

Kovack turned to the others and said, "Get the Hoofas down off the ship and pack them up. We cannot ride them in the sand. The weight will be too much, and they will sink. We will walk them out until the sand becomes firm."

Fig and Isa nodded and went in to get the Hoofas.

Kovack turned to Captain Maku and asked, "Captain, will you track Azdaja?"

"No, he had paid his debt to me and was free to leave if he wished. I wish him luck. It is not an easy road he chose."

Kovack nodded and turned to leave.

"Thank you for the adventure, I hope the remainder of your trip is as exciting," the captain said.

"I hope not," Kovack said without turning around. He walked into their room and looked around, only Fig's broken wagon remained. It had smashed into the wall in the crash and was not repairable. Fig would have to leave some of his things behind. Kovack sighed as he thought to himself. Why did he leave his forest? Then he smiled because he knew why, she was special.

10

The Tree Speak

Kovack joined the others at the Hoofas. "Each of you take a rein and lead a Hoofa. Kofang, you and Isa lead. Stay alert! The dock is half a day ahead, Let's go!"

They rounded the sand dunes staying close to the river as they walked. The sun was getting low in the sky when off in the distance, they could see many ships tied at the dock.

Kovack motioned for them to turn in away from the river and then he mounted the Hoofa and said, "The sand is firm enough now. Let's get some distance between us and that dock before we camp for the night."

Fig climbed up into his saddle, a bit nervous, he hadn't ridden on top before. Ynas climbed up followed by Isa on Kofang.

"Fig, follow close behind me, Ynas, take the rear." And with that, they darted off toward the sun. As the sun was disappearing off in the horizon, Kovack raised his hand and they all slowed to a stop. "We make camp there." He pointed to a tree line just off in the distance. "Hurry now before we lose our light." They raced to the tree line and slowed as they entered the forest.

"Fig, gather wood. We make a small fire. Isa, set up the fire ring." Kovack pulled down the bed rolls and laid them out under the canopy of the trees. Ynas cut up the roots and placed them in the pot with the berries and water. Fig returned with the dry wood and placed it in the small pit and ring of stones Isa had placed around it. Kovack started the fire as the last of the sun's light had faded.

"This feels like a safe place, the trees are happy here." Kovack looked relaxed.

"Good, now tell us a story. A story of...my father and how you knew him. You have been avoiding it for long enough. I need to know," Isa said sternly.

"Isa," Kovack sighed, "We are traveling to my old home. I guess I should tell you now." He paused and poked the fire with a stick. "I was the captain of the guard of Gosha. I met your father many years before the war. We fought in the arena together, as opponents, testing our strengths. We became friends, even as close as brothers. He was a brilliant fighter, extremely fast, but not quite as strong as Kovack. Kovack was nowhere as fast as he, but together, we were unstoppable...well, almost. The war started and we each were called back to our kingdom to fight. Many years passed and as the war neared its end, we met on the battlefield. Our armies combined strength overpowered the enemy. We fought side by side again, but in the fight, I was knocked unconscious and when I awoke, he was gone. I have no idea what happened. I returned to the Naslov kingdom as soon as I was able, but found that your mother had fallen on the battlefield and your Granny had taken you away to safety. I used the Tree Speak that your father had taught me to locate you and I have lived in the forest close by ever since."

"You have been watching over me this whole time!? Then why so gruff when we first met?"

"You did not need me yet, not till you called for me. I lost your father, I will not lose you. I see his abilities in you and more. Your mother was a great fighter also. You shall surpass them both."

"I do not feel like a fighter."

"That's ok, but do not limit yourself. Take in everything around you, feel it all. The fighter spirit in you protects all that you feel. You will fight for those who can't. I know why you like climbing in the trees. You feel free surrounded by all the living things there, more than on the ground. Your father was the same. Keep practicing, feel everything and everyone around you."

Isa could not hold back the tears as they flowed. She had never known her father or her mother. She walked out of the camp and climbed a tree. She settled in a high branch and cuddled Ono in her arms until she fell asleep.

Fig stayed quiet through the conversation. After Isa left, he walked up to Kovack and said, "It was hard when I lost my mother, give her some time."

"Yea, she will be ok," Kovack said as he doused the fire, and they all went to sleep.

In the morning light, Isa sat in the tree staring off into the distance. She felt the wind on her face and heard the leaves rustling around her.

"Isssaaa."

"What was that?!" she exclaimed and jumped down out of the tree. "Did you hear that?!"

"Hear what?" Fig asked as he rubbed his eyes.

"Someone called my name!" Isa answered.

"I didn't hear anything," Fig replied.

Isa explained, "That's cus you were asleep. Listen!" Isa looked over at Kofang. The hairs on his back were standing up. He was standing rigid with his nose down slightly and his head tilted to the side a bit as if to listen better. He was growling low.

"Quiet, Kofang, Listen!?" Isa commanded.

Kovack sat up and looked around. "Kovack sees nothing."

"Shh, not see, hear!" Isa said as she had her finger to her lip.

The wind rustled the leaves. The trees swayed back and forth.

"Isssaaa."

"There it is again, did you hear it!" Isa said excitedly.

They all looked at each other confused.

"No. We don't hear anything. That's because it is meant only for you, Isa," Ynas explained as she walked over to Isa. "Listen to everything around you. Walk out into the forest. Listen and learn the Tree Speak."

"It's the trees!!? I can hear the trees?!" Isa exclaimed and she turned and ran off into the forest. Kofang continued to growl and started to chase after Isa, but Kovack grabbed his harness and stopped him.

"Let her be. She needs to listen alone," Kovack said as he ran his hand through Kofang's back. "She needs to learn."

Kofang whimpered and stared after Isa.

Fig began setting out some food. "What is Tree Speak?"

"Everything around you is alive and has a voice, you must learn to listen," Ynas explained. "We as Naslov have learned to communicate with the Trees and plants as well as the animals of this world. When you open your mind and really listen, you can learn it too."

Fig paused for a moment. "And they really talk?"

"Not like you and I, you can hear it as a feeling inside," Ynas continued.

"I have studied many things and never heard of this. I would like to learn if I may," Fig said as he brought the bowl of food over and handed it to Ynas.

"Of course. We can try. However, not everyone can truly listen. It takes concentration and determination, but if you truly wish to learn, you will be able to overcome any obstacle. First will be, forget what you think you know. It will keep you from accepting what you will need to learn. Sit and meditate in the forest and practice listening. When you hear the trees calling, you have done it correctly."

"It is not so easy as you say," Kovack added

"Oh no, it will not be easy at all," Ynas said, "to unlearn something you believe in and accept something such as this is extremely difficult. The trees speak constantly, hearing them is the problem. The problem is not in your ears, it is in your mind. You can practice as we wait for Isa to return."

Fig finished his food and cleaned his plate. He was curious. He thought he was a good listener. He walked a short distance from the camp and sat next to a tree with his legs crossed. He folded his hands in front of him, closed his eyes and concentrated. He could hear the wind and the leaves rustling. What else? he thought.

"Fiiiggg."

Fig jumped up and ran to camp yelling, "I heard it, I heard it!"

Kovack came walking back to camp laughing. "Fig heard Kovack, "He was laughing so hard, he could hardly speak. "Keep trying, keep trying," Kovack said between bursts of laughter. "Kovack will not do that again."

Fig shook his head. "Yea, well you got me alright. It was a good one. When you're done laughing, will you help me practice?"

"Of course." Kovack took in a deep breath. "You must clear your mind. Now place your hand on the tree like this and listen. Hmm, they say that was a funny joke," Kovack chuckled.

"Yes, it was. Are they laughing too?" Fig said.

"No, the trees are not laughing…" Kovack said as he cleared his throat. Ok now, stay here, shut your eyes, and listen. I will go back to camp. Later, when Kovack returns, you can tell me what you can hear."

Fig placed his hand on the tree and closed his eyes, glancing back to see if Kovack had walked back to the camp. He breathed deep and concentrated.

The sun was high in the sky when Isa returned.

"How did it go?" Ynas asked.

"The trees didn't have much to say," Isa answered, "I felt a lot of different things, not sure how to make it all clear though."

"It will come with time, as you improve your listening," Ynas explained. "Fig is over there trying to improve his skills now."

"Really? Can he hear the trees?"

"Ask him, he has been there for hours, even after Kovack's little prank."

"Kovack pulled a prank on Fig? Oh No, I better go check on him." Isa walked over to Fig. "How's it going? Hear anything?"

Fig turned his head, "Isa? Your back. No, I can't hear anything. How did it go for you?"

"Don't be discouraged. Mine didn't go very well either. I can feel them and hear some, but not very clear yet. We can practice more together later, for now, why don't we get some food."

"Good idea."

Isa and Fig walked back to camp.

Kovack was loading the Hoofas. "We are getting a late start, you may practice more later, you need to get some food quickly before we ride."

Fig and Isa quickly ate their mid-day meal and got into their saddles. Kovack started out slowly watching the horizon as they rode. When he was sure no one had followed them, he turned deeper into the forest. There was no trail, and the trees were too thick to ride fast. Isa enjoyed taking it slower. She closed her eyes and let Kofang guide her as she felt the forest around her. The wind was cool on her face, the rustling of the leaves drowned out the other noises.

The forest opened and Kovack hollered, "Let's go!"

Isa snapped out of her concentration and grabbed the handles on the saddle tight as Kofang lunged forward into a full stride.

"A little warning next time, please," she said to Kofang as she leaned forward into the saddle. She thought she heard a little chuckle from Kofang.

"Not you too, Kofang, we don't need two pranksters among us."

Kofang nodded and ran even faster, passing Ynas, then Fig. He was closing in on Kovack and matched his speed as he came alongside. Isa glanced over at Kovack, then called out, "Come on Kofang, Let's show them speed!" Kofang leaped forward and disappeared into the trees ahead. Kovack just smiled and shook his head. They continued along until they caught up to Isa. She was stopped ahead and had dismounted. Isa was walking around through the trees. She asked, "Kovack, why do I sense sorrow in these trees?"

Kovack replied, "Kovack does too, something happened here. Kovack does not know what, be careful. We will travel slower and stay together. Keep a lookout for clues." Isa climbed back into her saddle, and they began riding slowly watching in all directions. Up ahead, the trees were all black and charred.

"Oh no!" Isa yelled, "this is the reason the trees are filled with sorrow. Who would have done such a thing!"

"Who, or what?" Kovack asked. "Lightning in a storm may cause such a fire, but this was not so recent as the storm we were in. If you wish to know, we look for clues. You may not like what you find."

Isa called to Kofang, and he leapt forward darting through the ash. She searched across the valley. Fig directed his Hoofa in the opposite direction and searched as well. Kovack closed his eyes. He could hear the cries of the charred trees. He knew how this had happened.

"I've found something!" yelled Isa.

There, next to her in the ground was a ring of rocks. She said, "Someone had a fire. They did not cover it. Do you think this started the fire?"

"It looks as though someone was careless," Kovack said, "many animals lived here among these trees. It will grow back, but it will take time."

"Why are people so careless?!" Isa said furiously, "this is our home, we ALL live here!"

"We cannot be responsible for other people, but hope they will be responsible for themselves," Ynas said as she came alongside Kofang on her Hoofa. "It is regrettable, but nothing we can do here for now but let it grow back. We should continue but be cautious. We may come across the people responsible."

"I hope we do!" Isa said as Kofang turned and began running to the other side of the burnt forest. The others turned their Hoofas and followed. Isa had tears coming down her cheeks as they rode. She could feel the sadness all around her. As she reached the green trees on the other side, she called to Kofang, who came to a stop and turned to look back. The whole valley was charred, but the green remained around it. From where she stood, she could see the desert beyond the trees. The area was still moist. The storm must have put out the fire. As bad as the storm seemed, she was very glad it had passed through the area. If it had not, the whole forest might have burnt down.

"Isa, are you alright?" Fig asked as he approached.

"I'll be ok, Fig," Isa sighed.

Isa turned Kofang back into the forest. She shut her eyes and listened as Kofang walked. She imagined the trees as they were before, green, and beautiful. She thought of how they would grow to be just as green and beautiful. She could feel the trees calming down as if they heard her. She opened her eyes and placed her hand on Kofang's shoulders and said, "We shall protect it all! Are you with me?"

Kofang raised his head and howled so loud it echoed across the forest. "Let them all know, we are here, and we will NOT allow this to happen again!" Kofang howled again. Isa yelled with him. Fig joined in.

Kovack and Ynas let them finish and continued through the forest. "No need to be careful, everyone knows we are here now," Kovack said as he chuckled. "We will need to find a place for the night soon. We will stop at the next clearing."

Isa stopped at the highest part of the hill. The trees were thinner there. She jumped off Kofang and walked up and put her arms around his neck, sinking her face into his fur. Kofang closed his eyes and they stood there awhile.

Fig entered the clearing and dismounted. He sighed, "I'm not used to riding, I'm sore all over."

"You get used to it," Kovack said as he entered the clearing. "We all deserve some rest after that ride."

They built a camp, and all sat down to eat.

"We should get an early start. Try to get some rest tonight," Kovack said after cleaning and putting his bowl away." He laid on his mat and stared up at the stars with thoughts of what lay ahead on his mind.

Fig and Isa walked over to a tree.

"Can you climb a tree well?" Isa asked as she looked up.

"Um...I haven't had a need to," Fig replied as he looked up. "It's so tall."

"The trees in my forest are much bigger. The branches stretch out far and are big enough to hold a small home. You can easily jump from branch to branch. These are too small and far apart to jump from tree to tree.

"Yea, but you have claws, I don't. I am not sure I can grip."

"I'll help you, I want to show you something." Isa started climbing the tree. When she got up to an upper branch, she lowered a rope and helped Fig up. From that point, Fig was able to climb up through the branches till they were at the top of the tree.

"Careful, these are thinner, and we will sway in the breeze," Isa said, "now look around." Both moons were just above the horizon. The smaller moon was set in the center of the bigger moon. "Doesn't it look like an eye, watching us from above?"

"Yea, but why does it feel so different up here from on the ground?" Fig asked.

"I always feel better in the trees, almost as if they are hugging me. You can see the whole valley from here. The black scar is not as big as it seemed before. See the river off in the distance? It seems like a sliver from here."

"It all looks so much more like my maps from here. I should take some sketches." Fig tied himself to the tree trunk and took out his parchment. "Good thing both moons are out, I can see pretty well." He sketched out the landscape, adding the river ahead and the mountains off in the distance to his left. "How far do you think those mountains are?"

"I think it would take many moonrises to get there," Isa said, "do you know what is there?"

"That is Mount Moraii, where my father is. From here we are about two moonrises from Gosha. I will add these sketches to my maps after we get there. There, that should do it," Fig said as he scanned the horizon to make sure he got everything.

He pointed. "Is that smoke?"

Isa turned her head and could barely make out the smoke.

"It's not far away, let's go." Isa jumped down through the branches and onto the ground.

"Hold on! I'm not as fast as you!" Fig yelled as he untied the rope and began climbing down.

Isa ran over to Kofang and nudged him. "Kofang, I need you, quietly though. There is smoke not far up ahead."

Kofang stood up and walked with Isa out of camp. They arrived at the tree just as Fig jumped down to the ground.

"Kofang, can you carry Fig and I to the smoke?"

Kofang nodded. They climbed on his back. Kofang shook his head as if to wake up and then began to run in the direction Isa indicated. After running for a good while, Kofang slowed and raised his head to sniff the air. He turned slightly and started to run again, stopping every so often to sniff again. He came to a stop and kneeled. Isa and Fig slid off him quietly. They walked through the trees to a clearing. There was a fire ring, still smoking and uncovered, but no one around.

"Help me put this out and cover it, Fig," Isa said as she took out her water jug and began pouring it over the fire.

Fig grabbed a branch and spread the embers while she poured. "Looks like they left this sunrise, and it has been smoldering all day. If a few leaves had blown in, this could have started another fire."

"I would like to catch up to these careless...whoever they are!" Isa said furiously.

Fig walked over to Kofang and climbed up on his back. "Let's get back to our camp, we will need some rest if we are going to catch up to them."

Isa looked around, making sure she didn't miss anything. "Alright, I have never seen anyone so careless!"

She walked over and climbed onto Kofang. Kofang stood up, turned around and headed back to their camp.

Fig admitted, "I am glad we brought Kofang, I would have gotten lost."

Isa laughed. "You're a map maker, how would you have gotten lost?"

"My father is the map maker. Part of map making is going into unknown territories. And um, well it all looks different when you're out in all this. Even with a map, I have never been out of town this far."

"It is fun, isn't it?" Isa asked.

"Yes, it really is." Fig nodded.

The moons were high in the sky by the time they reached their camp. Kofang slowed down and walked up to the edge of their camp. Isa and Fig slid off him and made their way into their beds. Ono snuggled up to Isa and they were all asleep before long.

Kovack and Ynas rose just before sunrise and quietly packed up their gear and prepared the morning meal. The smell woke Isa and Fig.

"Had a nice adventure last night?" Kovack asked as they sat up.

"You know?" Isa said.

Kovack gave Isa a look. "Of course, Kovack knows. Isa is not good enough at sneaking, remember the black bird?"

"Black bird?" Fig asked.

"Yes, I snuck off into the Dark Woods to find my family. I was attacked by a large black bird. It hit me in the shoulder. Kovack had seen me sneak off and hit the bird before it got me a second time."

Fig shook his head. "And after that, you still haven't learned. What if we had found who was responsible for that fire last night? What would you have done if they were there? You need to think more before you act, and who am I to speak? I went with you."

Isa turned to Kovack. "Kovack, we found a fire ring smoldering with hot coals. That could have started another fire through the trees. We need to find who is doing this and teach them a lesson."

"Kovack agrees. No one will be allowed to burn the trees. We will ride hard today and catch up to them. We leave as soon as Fig and Isa are ready."

Fig and Isa packed up and ate quickly. "Kofang, do you have the scent from the camp?" Isa asked. Kofang nodded, turned, and stepped in the direction they would be headed. Isa climbed on and Kofang walked forward slowly until everyone had mounted their Hoofas.

Isa looked back and after seeing they were all lined up, yelled, "Let's go!"

Kofang surged forward dodging trees back and forth. The trees were not as close together as before. The land dipped for a while, then rose higher. Isa could feel the beating of Kofang's heart. She leaned forward and closed her eyes. She felt his muscles flexing with each stride. She opened her eyes and stood up, placing a foot in front and behind the saddle and stretching her arms out wide to help her balance. Kofang did not slow down but steadied his stride. Isa moved her legs in unison with each stride, keeping herself steady above her waist. Isa rode like this for a while before sliding back down into the saddle.

Kovack shook his head and looked back at Ynas behind him. Ynas smiled. Fig followed behind Ynas. His riding skills had greatly improved, and he was easily keeping pace with the others. They rode on till the sun was getting low in the horizon when Isa saw smoke. She urged Kofang on faster until it was just ahead.

"Slow down Kofang," Isa said. "Good job, we found them." She stood up on Kofang's back and jumped up onto a branch. "Kofang, wait for the others, I will check it out and return here." Kofang turned his head back toward the way they came in and waited.

Isa climbed high up into the tree. From there she could see the camp a short distance ahead. She watched for a while. Two Goshan children were trying to start the fire. The leaves they put in the pit were making a lot of smoke but still no flames. There was a large beast tied to a tree, but she could see no one else. Isa climbed down and joined the others. After telling what all she saw, Isa looked at Kovack and asked, "What do we do?"

"We go talk to them. You say they look young, so keep calm," Kovack said and turned and walked toward their camp. Isa and Fig followed behind him, with Kofang and Ynas last.

Kovack entered the camp. "Need help with a fire?"

The Goshan children jumped and turned around. "Who are you?" the young boy shouted as he raised a stick with a charred end.

"I am Kovack, a fellow Goshan. This is Isa, Fig, Ynas, and Kofang."

The little girl screamed at the sight of Kofang.

The Goshan with the stick put his arm up in front of her and said, "I'll protect you, Miya." He pointed the stick at them. "Stand back!!"

Isa stepped forward. "We will not hurt you. Kofang is our friend."

She turned and motioned to Kofang. Kofang turned around and walked out of the camp. Isa walked slowly up to them and said, "See, Kofang listens to me. We are not here to hurt you, but I do want to ask you a question. Well, let's start with your name."

"My name is Bolva. This is my sister, Miya," said Bolva cautiously.

"Bolva, we are looking for someone who started a forest fire a few days ago," Isa said.

"We didn't start no fire!" Bolva exclaimed.

Ynas stepped forward and said, "Isa, please. Hello young ones. I am Ynas. Where are you from?"

Miya explained, "We came from a village down by the river. Raiders came and took everyone."

"Miya hush!! How do we know you are not raiders?" Bolva asked.

"I am too old to be a raider, young one," Ynas said, "but raiders, you say. Did you see which way they went?"

"They went from across the river before the water came," Bolva explained, "we hid till they were gone, and the river began to fill so they could not come back. We are headed to Gosha to ask the Queen for help."

"You can join us, we are also headed to Gosha," Ynas said, "you will be safe. For now, let Kovack show you how to start a fire."

The young boy watched as Kovack walked over and bent down. Without looking up, Kovack called out, "Come here, you cannot learn if you don't watch."

Bolva walked over to Kovack holding his sister's hand and pulling her with him. Kovack used his spark stones and started the fire. Then handed it to Bolva and said, "now you try."

Bolva tried hitting the stones together.

Kovack said, "A little more angle."

Bolva hit the stones together a few more times.

"Good." Kovack nodded. Bolva reached out to hand the stones back to Kovack. Kovack stood up and said, "Keep them, you can practice often, soon you will be as good as Kovack."

Bolva smiled and said, "Thank you." He turned to Miya. "Come, sit by the fire and keep warm."

Fig walked over and sat next to them and asked, "Do you mind?"

Miya shook her head. Fig pulled a toy out of his pocket and handed it to Miya. "If Bolva should get spark stones, you should get something too. Here."

Miya's eyes grew wide. "What is it?"

Fig explained, "You place it on a rock like this and spin it. See. Do you like it?"

Miya watched it spin until it wobbled and fell.

She said, "I do, may I try?"

"Of course, it takes practice, so keep trying," Fig said.

Miya placed her little fingers at the top and spun the toy. It fell off the rock. She frowned and picked it up and tried again, this time it spun with a wobble and fell.

Fig smiled and said, "Keep trying, you'll get it.

"Bolva, have you eaten?" Kovack asked.

"We ate at sunrise, I need to search for food," Bolva replied, "my Apon is great at digging up roots with his nose."

"Kovack has food, will you and your sister eat with us?"

Bolva sighed as he said, "Yea, I think it's better, Kovack. I do not know how to get to Gosha. My parents told me to follow the trail on the left side of this mountain and turn toward the sea and that trail would take me there. I can't keep Miya safe, as much as I want to. Can we go with you?"

"Yes Bolva, we will keep you safe. Your parents were correct. You will see Gosha from the other side of this mountain before we descend. It will be the safest path to the city. The river flows to the sea next to Gosha, but after the trip we took, I would rather walk. Your beast is not fast, and it will take us a bit longer to get there, but that's ok."

"Look, Look! I did it!" Miya yelled.

The toy was spinning nicely on the rock. Bolva smiled for the first time in a long time. They shared a meal and Fig entertained Miya with a few more toys. After they ate, they rolled out the bedding and everyone went to sleep. Miya lay close to Bolva on the opposite side of the fire from everyone else.

Kovack was the first to rise. But this morning, he took a walk around the camp peering over the valley below. There were no signs of anyone following them. Who were these raiders? The Arena had not operated in many seasons. Perhaps he should have talked with Eber some more, maybe he would know.

Isa walked up behind Kovack. "Ha, in the sunrise, my shadow is as long as yours!"

"That is only because Kovack sits." Kovack chuckled. "How are you feeling lil one?"

"From the highest tree in my forest, I could not see half as far as here. I never imagined how big the world is. I feel so amazing, yet so small. Thank you for bringing me."

"Isa was meant to go, Kovack is only an escort. When you meet the queen, you will see."

They just watched as the sun rose behind them, lighting up the land in front of them. The desert seemed to glow in the morning light. Isa saw more dark clouds far off in the distance. "Do not worry lil one. The dark clouds do not cross this mountain. We will be on the other side before they reach here."

Fig walked up. "Wow, that looks amazing!"

They stayed till the sun had fully risen and the morning glow had faded, then walked back to their camp. Bolva and Miya were rolling up their bedding and packing Apon. Apon was as large as Kofang, but heavier built, with short hair and a large shovel shaped nose. A tusk protruded up from his bottom lip on each side of his mouth.

After packing and eating, they all mounted their animals. Isa called to Kofang, who bounded into camp, and she climbed into her saddle. Miya's eyes were wide with astonishment. She couldn't believe Isa could ride on Kofang.

"Bolva, do you see how we cooled and covered the fire?" Isa asked.

"Yes, why? It would have burned out," Bolva replied.

"Come with me." Isa turned Kofang and headed to the spot they had watched the sunrise. Bolva turned Apon and followed.

Isa waited for Bolva to reach the area. She pointed out to the forest, "Bolva, see that black scar running through the forest?"

"Yes."

"That was from your fire a few moonrises ago. If the storm had not put it out, it would have been a lot worse. Fig and I cooled and covered your last fire ring. You need to be more careful."

Bolva looked in astonishment, then exclaimed, "But why didn't it burn out?

"Fire can smolder for a long time. If you don't cover it and leaves or twigs blow into it, it will reignite and without you there, that is what happens."

"I will be more careful. I can't believe it did all that," Bolva said as his eyes began to tear.

Isa said sternly, "What is done cannot be undone. But we can learn from it. I hope you have."

"I have," Bolva said.

"Me too," Miya said.

"Good, now let's join the others."

They turned and walked back to camp where everyone was waiting. Isa looked over at Kovack and nodded. Kovack returned the nod and they all followed Kofang down towards the trail.

11

On to Gosha

Kofang wanted to run, but Isa held him back. "Sorry Kofang, but Apon cannot go any faster. I wish he could."

They reached the highest part of the trail and began the descent. With the sun behind them, they could see the great city of Gosha glistening off in the distance.

"Wow, would you look at that!" exclaimed Isa. "From here, it looks like a white jewel set between the forest and the waters."

"That, Isa, is the Sea of Izvan," Fig said as he rode up alongside Isa. "There's no end to it. At least as far as we know. No one who has gone beyond that horizon has ever returned."

"I guess it's a good thing I don't plan on taking a ship again anytime soon." Isa smiled and looked at Fig. "Is that a village I see at the base of the mountain?"

"Yes, I think it would be a welcomed place to stay the night," Fig said as he turned to Kovack and pointed out the village. Kovack nodded. They headed towards the village and stopped at the edge of it.

"Kovack will go and see if I can find a place to stay for the night. Wait for me." He dismounted and looked at Isa.

"I will this time, really," Isa replied reluctantly.

The town was busy with people closing their shops and bedding their animals for the night. No one noticed Kovack as he walked down the street and into the Inn. The Hostess' was busy writing in the daily log and looked up at the sound of Kovack's footsteps.

"Do you have rooms available?" Kovack inquired. "It's seven of us and four beasts."

"I do. Seven, you say?" The lady peered at him. "For seven, that would be at least three rooms."

"And baths are included with the rooms?" Kovack asked.

"Of course. There are two tubs set upstairs, I will begin to warm the water after you pay for the rooms."

Kovack handed her money and said, "Do we take the animals out back?"

The hostess replied, "Yes, I will have my son bring them food and water."

"Thank you," Kovack said as he turned and walked out the door.

Most of the shops were closed by now. The shop at the far end of the street was busy with people laughing and drinking. Kovack felt it was safe enough there. He walked back to the others. "Isa didn't take off? I am surprised." He chuckled.

"I don't always run off." Isa said as everyone turned their heads and looked at her. "Well...not always, but a few times maybe."

"Yea, a few times," he repeated as he shook his head. He took his hoofa by the reins and walked it into town. The others followed with Kofang trailing behind. Kovack tied the three hoofas and Apon up behind the Inn and walked around to the front. Kovack, Isa, Fig, Ynas, Bolva, Miya and Kofang walked into the Inn. The hostess looked up and yelled at the sight of Kofang.

Miya walked forward, "It's ok, he's our friend."

"Oh no no no, he can't stay in here!" The hostess stammered, "Friend or not, no beasts in here!"

"He is no beast. He is my friend, and a hero!" Isa exclaimed, "he has saved my life more than once."

"I am glad he has, but rules are rules," The Hostess said. "He will need to stay out in the back."

"If he goes, I go!" Isa said boldly.

Kofang pushed his nuzzle into Isa's side and turned to leave, as if to say, "It's ok." Isa watched as he walked quietly out the door. Then she turned and glared at the Hostess.

"I am sorry, young lady, but he would frighten anyone that sees him in here," the hostess said in the most sincere way she could. "Here are your keys. I will warm the water and bring it up to you shortly."

Isa turned and stormed up to her room. Ynas and Miya followed her. Fig, Kovack, and Bolva took the other room.

"Well, to be honest, I am not sure I was up to giving Kofang a bath tonight anyway," Fig said as he prepared his bed.

Kovack laughed. "Yea, that was an adventure, wasn't it?"

Bolva looked confused, so Fig told him the story as Kovack prepared for his bath. Each took their turn taking a bath and soon they were all asleep.

Shortly after sunrise, Fig woke to find Kovack gone and Bolva turned sideways on his bed still fast asleep. Fig shook him a little and called out, "Bolva, come on, wake up." Bolva's eyes fluttered. "Bolva, wake up, come on, the others are leaving."

Bolva sat up fast, turned his head toward Fig, then his eyes closed, and he fell back into his bed. Fig grabbed the side of the bed and pulled and Bolva rolled out onto the floor with a thud.

"Ow! Why did you do that?" Bolva said in a half groan.

Fig replied, "Cus everyone else is already up, let's go!" He walked out of the room and downstairs.

Bolva got up slowly and looked around the room for his clothes. He grumbled, "First time I've been in a bed in weeks, could've let me sleep." He made his way downstairs.

The hostess had set food out on the table. He took a few rolls and walked outside. He looked up and down the road as he took a bite of the roll, but he didn't see anyone from his group. He shrugged his shoulders and went out back. Apon was busy eating and the hoofas were still in their stalls, so Bolva decided to stay there with Apon and wait for the others.

Fig found Kovack walking down the street, checking the vendor's merchandise. As they approached a weapon material shop, Fig tapped Kovack on the arm and entered the shop. Kovack walked in behind him. The shop had strips of leather hanging in the back, bins of raw metal lined the walls and ropes of different lengths hung above them.

"Look at these, Kovack, little round metal pellets," Fig said. "Hmmm…I have an idea. Can I get a few things? I lost most of my stuff in the ship crash."

"Pick what you need, but keep it light," Kovack answered.

Fig went through bin after bin until he had what he needed. "Ok, I'm finished. This will do nicely."

"What's it for?" Kovack asked.

"You'll see. I'll need a hot fire though. I hope I can use one in Gosha."

They paid for the material and walked out of the shop.

Kovack looked down the street. "If you're up, then everyone is. We should get back to the Inn."

"Yea, I tried to wake Bolva, I hope he got up," Fig replied. The streets were filling with more people.

"Kovack does not like it so busy."

They started walking back to the Inn.

Ynas and Miya had joined Bolva at the Hoofas.

"There you are," Ynas said as Kovack rounded the corner. "Where's Isa? She was gone before I woke up."

"Kovack is sure Isa is with Kofang. We can pack up and find her there," Kovack said.

They packed the animals and climbed in the saddles. Kovack headed toward where they entered the town and led the group back to the trail. They turned toward Gosha without making a sound. Before long, Kofang came bounding out of the forest carrying Isa.

"Isa slept well I hope?" Kovack asked.

"I did. Ono and I prefer the trees to a stuffy room." Isa smiled.

"Ok then, scout ahead, should be no trouble, but check," Kovack said.

"Got it," Isa said and then called out to Kofang and ran ahead.

The rest of the group walked the same speed as Apon, who barely walked faster than any of them could even without a hoofa.

12

The Goshan Kingdom

The trail was wide enough that the tree branches did not close overhead and it grew wider as they walked. They noticed the ground was smoother and firmer than before. Soon they came upon a wood post in the trail as it split in four directions. Isa was looking at the signs on the post as she circled around it while sitting on Kofang.

Isa shouted, "Look Kovack, Maplehaven is that way! I remember Maplehaven. It does not give directions to Oakheart though." She pointed. "It says that way to Gosha."

"Lead the way, lil one," Kovack said.

They continued down the trail toward Gosha occasionally passing travelers. The forest opened up to houses setting far apart with fields in between. Fences kept the larger animals close to the houses. Piles of hay were scattered across the fields. As they passed the fields, the houses were much closer together, and larger. Young Goshan children were running around playing. They stopped and watched when they saw Kofang walking down the trail. Some of them ran into their houses and shut the doors. The trail became a road paved in white stone. The houses here were even larger than the previous ones.

They came upon a large wall with a gate made of huge wooden beams. On each side was a guard in shiny silver armor. Both guards glared at the group as they passed.

The guard on the right looked down at Kofang and said, "What is a beast like this doing in our great city? You should go back to your forest, lil dog!"

"Kofang is no lil dog!" Isa yelled.

Kovack raised his hand to quiet Isa, then turned towards the guard and asked, "Is that how you welcome travelers to your great city? What would your captain say if your armor was tarnished?"

The guard retorted, "I would be severely punished, dismissed and sent home until I had it as shiny as it is now."

"And how much more important is your character than your armor?"

The guard bowed his head in shame as Kovack turned his head away and continued walking into the city.

All the buildings' walls and roads were made of the white stone. Arched holes were scattered throughout the walls providing light to the rooms inside. The stones were rougher cut than in the Tobu Kingdom with wider gaps in between each stone. They turned and headed up an arched road that led to the palace. They stopped at the highest point of the arch and dismounted as three guards approached them.

The guard in the center put up his hand and said, "I am Mithril, Captain of the Guard here in Gosha. What business do you have here?"

Kovack bowed and said, "I am Kovack, previous Captain of the Guard of this great city. We have been sent by King Beyla to speak with Queen Shea. The two young ones, Bolva and Miya, need your assistance with raiders who attacked their village by the river and took their families."

"Kovack?! I was still young, but I remember you," Mithril said, "no one has heard from you since shortly after the war. I am curious to hear your story, but first we will take care of these young ones." He motioned to the guards standing next to him.

They took Apon by the reins and led him down the road to the stables as Bolva and Miya followed. "Now then, you wish to speak with Queen Shea. She doesn't see visitors anymore. Who are these Naslov with you?" He looked at Isa. "And this one rides a Draufganger?"

"She will see Kovack," Kovack explained, "this is Isa, granddaughter of Ynas, whom your queen knows well and the young Goshan here is our friend, Fig."

"The Red-haired warrior?" Mithril asked with surprise, "I have heard the rumors. I will speak with the Queen and send someone to take your hoofas to the stables. Please wait here."

A few moments later, three young Goshan men approached them and took the hoofas down to the stables.

Ono seemed uneasy sitting on Isa's shoulders. Kofang kept glancing back and forth nervously. He remembered the last time he was in a city, they threw him in the arena.

Mithril knocked on the Queen's door. "My Queen, Kovack has returned and has requested to see you. He has brought the Red-haired warrior with him along with her grandmother, Ynas."

The Queen's handmaiden opened the door. Mithril stepped in. Queen Shea looked surprised. "Kovack has returned, and the Red-hair warrior is with him? That makes sense. Her father and Kovack were close friends. Place dinner settings at my table and bring them in."

"The Red-hair warrior, Isa, rides a Draufganger," Mithril added.

"Is it tame?"

"It is."

"Do as Isa wishes with it." She motioned for her handmaiden to close the door.

Mithril turned and walked back to the group. "You can come with me. I will show you to your rooms. Please wash up, you will be joining Queen Shea for dinner."

Mithril walked them down a long hall. "Here is your room Ynas. Across the hall will be your room, Isa. Kovack, you may take that room and finally Fig, over there. I will have warm water brought to your rooms shortly."

"And what about Kofang? Where will he sleep?" Isa asked.

"Where would you like him to sleep?"

"He can stay in my room, if that is ok."

"That will be fine. Now, dinner will be ready by sunset, please be ready." Mithril turned and walked away.

The smell of the food carried down the hallway into their rooms.

"Oh, I just realized how hungry I am," Fig said as he opened the door and walked into the hallway. He knocked on Isa's door, then walked down to Kovack's room.

"You guys ready? I'm hungry, let's go." He walked over to knock on Ynas door as the door opened.

"I am ready Fig, no need to knock." Ynas winked at him.

Isa was next out of her room with Kofang. Kovack walked out of his room patting down his shirt.

"Who is that?" Isa said jokingly, "wow, you look almost handsome."

"Very funny. Kovack hasn't seen the queen in a very long time."

"You're nervous?"

"No, Kovack just wants to look good."

"Uh huh," Isa said suspiciously.

"Is anyone else hungry? Let's go eat!" Fig said as he motioned with his hands.

They walked down the hall and into the dining room. The walls were covered in tapestries of many colors. In the center of the large room sat a long table with many dishes of food on it. At each of the hand carved wooden chairs was a plate, a bowl, a cup, and silverware. From the ceiling hung a large chandelier with candles flickering. Each of them took a seat at the table. There was even a bowl of food set for Kofang near Isa's seat. After they settled down from admiring the room and all the food, one of the servants called out to the Queen. Shea entered the room from the right. She was tall and had light skin with blue eyes and golden blonde hair that hung down to her waist. She wore a gown of white, studded with diamonds down the length of the collar that flowed down and attached to her waist.

"Welcome, all of you, to Gosha," Queen Shea began.

They all jumped up out of their chairs and walked over to the Queen and bowed.

"It is nice to see you again Kovack, Ynas." She bowed her head in acknowledgment. "And this is Isa and Kofang? Oh, and who is this?"

"This is Ono, he has been my friend for as long as I can remember," Isa said as she reached out her arm and Ono walked down to her hand.

Shea put her hand up to Ono and let him smell her. After Ono was satisfied that the Queen was a friend, he returned to Isa's shoulder.

"I see that you have a good group of friends," Shea said, "please take your seats and enjoy the food."

Everyone returned to their seats and bowed their head to offer up a short prayer for the food. After the blessing, Shea looked over to Kovack and asked, "Where have you been all this time, Kovack?"

"Kovack left for the forest near Oakheart where Isa was raised in order to watch over her after her father disappeared in the final fight of the war," Kovack explained.

"I remember that Battle well. We lost many good warriors in that War. We can speak of those things another time, for now, eat and enjoy the evening."

They told Shea of the adventures they had on the way there. The ride on the ship, Kofang's bath, Their time in the Tobu kingdom and even Dark Woods. Shea listened for hours as each gave their versions on how things happened.

After they finished, Shea stood up and said, "It looks like we have some work to do. Training begins tomorrow in the Arena. I expect all of you there except Fig. Fig, you may go to the library and study. I believe you will find what we have most useful on your journey to come. I will prepare a letter to grant you permission to enter Mt Moraii on behalf of your father. Sleep well, all of you." The queen turned and left the room.

They all stood up and headed for their rooms. Isa was so excited, how could she sleep now? Fig and Isa talked all the way back to their rooms. Kovack and Ynas were quiet. They knew what the arena meant.

Just after breakfast, they met in the corridor.

"Do your best today, Isa, I will see you after. I'm off to the library," Fig said as he spun and walked down the corridor.

"Enjoy the Library, Fig." She turned toward Kovack. "Kovack, what's a library?"

Kovack laughed and said, "A library has many books and scrolls of knowledge of things that have happened before. If you forget a mistake that was made before, you may make the same one again. Improving your mind is very important."

"I can see how that makes sense, but I like doing things more than reading."

"As does Kovack, but many great things I've learned are only in books."

"Maybe I'll go later and visit Fig," Isa said.

"Hurry now, we don't want to be late," Kovack said and motioned to Isa.

They walked down the arched road and through the city to the arena. No one was in the streets. All the shops were closed.

Isa looked around. "Where's everyone?"

"Already at the arena, waiting for us." Kovack answered.

They turned the next corner and saw the huge white building in front of them, the door was twice as tall as any Goshan. They walked through the doors and into the center of the arena where the queen was waiting.

Shea looked over at Kofang. "You were raised as a beast, but in your eyes, I see more. Why are you here? You were not forced to come."

"Kofang is my friend!" Isa exclaimed.

"Quiet! Let him answer me," Shea shouted back.

"But he can't speak," Isa explained.

"You should know better than that by now. Have you not heard him?" The queen said.

Isa thought for a moment and said, "I do remember, all things can speak if you listen."

"Yes, now quiet, you cannot listen while you're talking. Now Kofang, answer me. Why are you here? Speak up!" Shea jabbed Kofang with her staff. He growled and jumped back. "Very well then, if you will not speak, then FIGHT!" Shea swung her staff over her head and then down across Kofang's head, knocking him across the ground and into the far wall. Everyone jumped back, Kovack put his arm down in front of Isa, restraining her.

"Why are you doing this?!" Isa yelled.

"You must trust her. Stay out of it and watch," Kovack said.

Shea charged at Kofang, landing a blow to the wall as Kofang dodged. Kofang darted across the arena with amazing speed. He turned and charged at Shea. Shea stood firmly with her staff held in both hands horizontally at her chest. As he drew close and bit, she pushed the staff into his mouth and rolled back, throwing him far across the arena.

"Let me see into your mind!" she yelled as he landed.

Kofang charged again. She used her staff to knock him to the side. Over and over, he charged, with each attack easily being deflected. Kofang looked across at Shea. He saw into her eyes. He could hear her voice in his head. He shook his head and charged again. She knocked him down and he landed on his side. Her voice became louder in his head. He shook his head again as he thought. What was she doing? He is a beast, was a beast, Isa is a friend, Kovack is a friend. His thoughts were cloudy. Ono is annoying, Ynas is old. He turned and stumbled away from Shea.

I must not let her in. Get out of my mind! Kofang thought as he charged Shea again, this time grabbing her staff in his mouth and throwing her over his head. Shea landed on her feet and knelt down.

"Hear me now, Kofang," Shea yelled, "and clear your mind!"

Kofang shook his head again and charged. As he drew close, Shea drove the end of her staff directly into his forehead. Kofang's mind grew clear, and he could understand now. He was more than a beast, he was a friend and a hero to many.

Shea walked over to Kofang, knelt down, and looked him straight in his large, yellow eyes and said, "Do you know who you are now, great warrior?"

"Yes, thank you for opening my mind," Kofang answered.

"What?! Kofang, I can hear you. How is this possible?" Isa exclaimed.

"I am glad you can hear me now," Kofang said.

The Queen explained, "All things are possible to you when you open your mind. Most important is to know who you are, not what others tell you you are. I could see Kofang struggling. All his life, people called him a beast. He knew nothing else until you came along. Kofang is much more, but he must believe it. Tomorrow, we will continue our training. Until then, rest and enjoy the remainder of the day." Shea turned and walked out of the arena.

Isa looked up at Kovack confused. Kovack looked down at Kofang and asked, "Are you all right?"

"Yes, she hits hard, but I have been beaten harder in my life," Kofang answered.

"You were not forced to come with us, but I am glad you decided to," Kovack said.

"I found you interesting, that's all," Kofang walked out of the arena and back to his room.

Isa still looked confused, but she didn't say a word. She slowly started walking to her room with Kovack as the sky grew darker.

"Kovack?" she asked.

"Yes?"

"What just happened?"

"Shea used her connection to the diamond. She can see into a person's mind and even help purify it if they are willing. It is natural to resist the process as Kofang tried, so she had to help him a little."

"Help a little? She attacked him!"

"The Queen knows what she is doing. She can see what we cannot."

"What do you think she sees in me?"

"She sees you, even better than you see you. We will get some rest. I believe tomorrow will be a long day. When she says training, she really means it."

"After what I saw, I believe it. It looks like we're in for a rough time here Ono," said Isa.

Ono whimpered and snuggled closer around Isa's neck as they walked back to their rooms. Ynas was asleep already as Isa quietly opened the door and made her way to her bed. Her mind raced with thoughts of the day ahead. Ono crawled onto her chest and began humming. This calmed her mind and Isa fell asleep.

Isa woke to a loud horn. "What's that!?" She said as she jumped out of bed, dressed quickly, and ran out to the hall. The others were already there.

"What's that horn blowing about?" Isa asked.

"That is the call to begin training," explained Kovack. "Let's go. We are wanted in the arena now."

Kofang growled, "I can't wait for another round."

"I am not ready!" Isa exclaimed. "What about breakfast?"

"Eat on the way, Ynas is already there," Kovack said.

They made their way to the arena. Shea was sitting up in her chair viewing from above. Mithril was sitting next to her.

As they walked into the arena, Shea stood up and announced, "Begin!"

Mithril jumped down into the arena with a powerful leap and charged toward Kovack. Kovack pulled his axe out just in time and blocked Mithril's attack. The impact sent Kovack flying across the arena.

Isa jumped toward Mithril as another axe landed into the ground in front of her, stopping her in her tracks.

"This is a one-on-one fight, Isa!" said the Queen, after throwing the axe. "Kovack, grab your old weapon!" Shea commanded.

Isa glared up at Shea, then looked over at Kovack. Kovack got to his feet.

Mithril charged again, swinging his axe over his head. Kovack grabbed Mithril's axe handle as it came down above his head. He looked into Mithril's eyes and threw him down to the right. Mithril rolled, jumped up onto his feet and charged, swinging his axe again. Kovack pulled his club out and blocked each swing, stepping back with each blow. Mithril thrust upward to knock Kovack off balance. As Kovack stumbled backwards, Mithril hit him in the chest as hard as he could. Kovack fell backwards next to the axe lodged in the ground. Mithril swung his axe down and as his axe fell, Kovack pulled his old axe out of the ground just in time to block the hit. Isa saw a dim blue flash of light. Mithril kept swinging his axe. Kovack kept blocking each swing as the blue light grew brighter with each hit and surrounded Kovack.

"Why don't you fight back?!" Mithril yelled. Kovack stood up thrusting his axe into Mithrils chest and the flash of blue light knocked Mithril across the arena.

"Enough!" called out Shea.

Ynas walked over to heal Mithril.

Shea exclaimed, "You remember who you are, Kovack. The Sapphire accepts you once again. Now rest for the remainder of the day. Kofang and I will fight next."

Shea walked down into the arena and checked on Mithril first and then Kovack. She joined Kofang in the center of the arena. She knelt down and said, "Here is a gift, Kofang. Wear it well." She placed the chest plate of armor embedded with a black gem over Kofang's head and buckled it snug at his shoulders. Shea explained, "Embedded in this armor is obsidian, the gem of stealth and speed. You cannot use it if your mind is not clear. Clear all your thoughts and concentrate. Now, shall we begin?" She stepped back and spun her staff.

Kofang drew back into a crouch, ready to leap. He lunged at Shea. She stepped aside and dodged his attack easily.

"Come now Kofang, do not disappoint me."

He slid and spun around, lunging again but faster this time. Shea dodged and hit him on his hindquarter. He let out a yelp and turned again. He came in zig zagging faster than before. Shea dodged once again, landing a blow on his head. Kofang's anger was sweeping through him. He could not let this lady beat him.

"You will not lose to me, you will lose to yourself!" Shea exclaimed. "You cannot win with anger. Now calm yourself and concentrate."

Kofang lowered his head. He could smell everyone. Concentrate, feel them, feel everything, he thought to himself. He breathed deep, raised his head, howled, and let go of all his anger. He looked back at Shea growling as a black light began to surround him and charged. He vanished in front of her, leaving only a black flash. He appeared on the opposite side of the arena and disappeared again. Shea was sent flying backwards. She somersaulted, landed crouched down and plunged her staff into the ground sliding back to a stop. Black flashes of light appeared in different areas across the arena.

What hit her? Isa wondered. She tried hard to follow Kofang, but he was too fast.

Kofang appeared in front of Shea. He bit down on her staff as she blocked, then, in an instant, he was behind her.

He is moving too fast, Isa thought, as she squinted trying to follow the fight.

Shea was barely blocking Kofang's charges, who was getting even faster.

"Enough!" she yelled. She plunged her staff into the ground filling the arena with a white flash, using her connection with the diamond. Kofang appeared in front of Shea, panting.

Shea nodded her head. "Well done, Kofang, the obsidian accepts you."

Kofang's eyes grew dark, Isa ran over to him as he collapsed to the ground.

Shea looked over at Isa and said, "He will be alright, he just needs rest. Most people will go through their whole life not really knowing who they are. You have your granny, Kofang had no one. Now, he has you." Shea turned and began walking out of the arena.

"WAIT! I challenge you!" Isa yelled, "you fought my friend, now fight me!"

Shea turned, looked at Isa and said, "You are not ready."

"I am ready!" Isa exclaimed, "Kofang is hurt and Mithril attacked Kovack. I do not understand your training."

"Very well. If you cannot wait," Shea said and walked to the middle of the arena. Isa stood opposite of her.

They waited for Kovack to carry Kofang out of the arena. Isa took her stance and glared at Shea. Shea stood there calm and ready. Isa charged at her chest with her weapons out to the side, swinging them across as she closed the gap between them. Shea stepped to the side and thrust her hand up from below Isa catching her in her gut knocking the wind out of her. Isa hit the ground, gasping for air. She turned, caught her breath, and concentrated. Her blades began to glow red as she prepared to charge.

"There is fire in you, Isa," Shea said, "do not let it cloud your mind."

Isa charged toward Shea, swinging her blades in a fury. Shea blocked the blows one after the other.

"You have connected to the ruby, Acacia taught you this, but cannot use its full power as you are. You are confused and struggling because your friends are hurt. Clear your mind!" Shea dropped her staff and used her hands to counter Isa's blows. She stepped in and placed the palm of her hand on Isa's forehead sending visions of the war through Isa's mind. Isa stumbled back and fell to her knees.

"What did you do to me?!"

"I have shown you why you are here. The aftermath of the war resulted in the creation of the four kingdoms. Many people suffered great losses to create a peaceful world. Kovack and Ynas were no exception. We cannot forget where we came from, or we will repeat it. My king is dead, and Beyla was poisoned. Peace is being threatened and we need you to fight this rising darkness."

"How do I fight a darkness I do not know?"

"Remember the things your granny and Kovack have taught you. You will identify the darkness and fight to keep Andalusia safe, teach and encourage others to do the same. It will take everyone working together to maintain that peace."

"I'm not sure I can."

"Then who will?" Shea asked and turned and left the arena.

Isa, still on her knees in the center of the arena, placed her hands over her face and started crying. How could anyone do such terrible things to each other? She felt so overwhelmed by these visions of the war.

Ynas walked over, knelt beside her, placed her hand on her back and said, "I never told you of the war, because I did not want you to feel how you are feeling now."

"Was this how my mother and father died?"

"Yes, losing my daughter crushed my fighting spirit and I lost my connection to the ruby. It is why I took you and your sister to our village and raised you there. Now that you know, what can I do to help you understand?"

"I'm not sure I'll ever understand. It's pointless. You taught me to value life and everything opposite of war."

"Not everyone believes as we do," explained Ynas.

"I need some time alone, granny. I'll be ok." Isa got up slowly and walked out of the arena.

Ynas waited until Isa was gone before going back to the palace. She knocked on Kovack's door. "Enter," Kovack said quietly and Ynas walked in.

Kofang was recovering on his bed and Kovack was sitting beside him.

"How's he doing?" she asked.

"Just needs time," Kovack answered.

"Shea was a bit rough on him."

"Shea knows what she is doing."

"I don't agree with her showing Isa the images of the war," Ynas said. "I have been protecting her all her life."

"Maybe you protected her too much," Kovack said as he stroked Kofang's fur.

"Maybe."

"We don't want to see another war start again. Isa must understand what we went through."

Meanwhile, Isa was standing out on the palace balcony, still in a daze from the arena, staring out at the sea.

"What do you see?" a voice came from behind her. Isa turned and saw Shea walking out onto the balcony.

"What do you mean?"

"What do you see?" Shea pointed at where Isa was staring.

"I don't know." Isa shrugged. "I guess I see a ship off in the distance and the moon beginning to rise."

"I see peace and calm, the wind causing ripples on the water as it reflects the moon's light." Shea placed her hands on the railing. "How each of us views the same things will be different, but who is correct? Your own perception will change over time. I will remove from your mind the images of war but keep those feelings close to your heart and never forget them. No one should suffer like that ever again." Shea placed her hand on Isa's forehead and with a flash of light, the visions of the war disappeared.

"You would do well to study in the library with Fig for a while. When you feel ready, you may join me in the arena." As Shea turned to leave, she said, "And, your father did not die in the battle that day.

About the Author

Darren Mitchell was born in Michigan, one of six children. When their apartment burned down, he and his family moved to Texas. After his mom separated from his stepdad, they moved to California.

Darren married young and had three children. He began a career as an electrician and worked his way up to superintendent, eventually relocating to San Jose.

Soon after getting divorced, Darren decided to write a story for his daughter. When family members read the incomplete manuscript, they urged him to publish it. He decided to submit it for publishing, and this began his career as an author.